Marrying the Wrong Earl

Lords AND Ladies IN Love

THE SERIES

Marrying the Wrong Earl

Lords AND Ladies IN Love

THE SERIES

Callie Hutton

Entangled Publishing, LLC
2614 South Timberline Road
Suite 109
Fort Collins, CO 80525
Visit our website at www.entangledpublishing.com.

Scandalous is an imprint of Entangled Publishing, LLC.

Edited by Erin Molta
Cover design by Erin Dameron-Hill
Cover art from RomanceNovelCovers.com

Manufactured in the United States of America

First Edition April 2017

SCANDALOUS

To all those who love their fur babies more than anything else.

Chapter One

Lady Arabella Danvers stared in horror as the Earl of Pembroke groaned and slid his vast body off the settee, landing with a thump onto one knee. He took her hand in his fleshy, sweaty one. "My lady—"

She sucked in a breath. "No, please, my lord. Do rise. Sit alongside me." She patted the settee, frantic to keep him from proposing. She'd known for some time what his intentions were but had hoped her lack of interest would have dissuaded him. Of course, she'd been well trained in how to word a refusal-of-marriage offer, but each time she'd had to do it, she'd suffered for days afterward seeing the pain of rejection in the gentleman's eyes.

"I must say this, Lady Arabella. I have admired you for some time now. You must know of my interest—"

"Perhaps I should send for more tea…" She attempted to tug her hand loose from his grip, to no avail. Her mother had left the room several minutes ago, leaving her not properly chaperoned, so apparently, Pembroke's fumbling attempt at a proposal was not a surprise to Mother.

"I hold you in a great deal of esteem." He continued on as if she hadn't spoken. "I would like at this time to ask you—"

"My lady?" Arabella breathed a sigh of relief as the butler, Tavers, entered the drawing room. "Lady Elizabeth and Miss Caroline Davis have come to call."

She smiled brightly at Lord Pembroke. "Perhaps you should rise, my lord."

He glowered at the butler then gave Arabella a wan smile. "Yes, yes, of course. I will continue this another time." He awkwardly shifted his girth to stand but instead fell halfway, practically landing on her.

"Lady Arabella, how wonderful to see you." Lady Elizabeth and her cousin, Miss Caroline Davis, glided into the room. Pembroke rearranged himself, red faced and puffing, attempting to regain his dignity. Arabella hopped up to greet her guests. The three kissed the air next to each other's cheeks, exclaiming over gowns and bonnets. No one seemed to notice Lord Pembroke, who gave a soft cough.

"Oh dear, my lord, I did not see you there." Lady Elizabeth gave him a slight curtsy, as did Miss Caroline, who murmured, "My lord."

"Good afternoon, ladies." He turned to Arabella. "I will leave you now to visit with your friends. May I have the pleasure of escorting you on a drive tomorrow afternoon?"

Lady Elizabeth and Miss Caroline both turned to Arabella with raised eyebrows.

"Yes, indeed. Lady Arabella would love a ride tomorrow afternoon, wouldn't you, dear?" Arabella's missing mother, Lady Melrose, hurried into the room, all sunshine and happiness.

"Actually, Mother, I had planned to…" She halted, unable to think fast enough.

Mother jumped right in. "Nonsense, a ride in the park would be just the thing. You spend far too much time doing whatever it is you normally do in the afternoons." She took Lord Pembroke's arm and walked him out of the room, her voice fading as she chatted away.

"Lord Pembroke?" Lady Elizabeth adjusted her skirts as she settled on a chair across from the settee where Arabella sat. "I had no idea."

"There is no idea. I know the man intends to propose, but I will not be accepting." Arabella filled teacups for herself and her two visitors. "Although I am not foolish enough to want love in a marriage, I would at least prefer to *like* the man I'll spend the rest of my life with." She shuddered as she took a sip of her tea. "And I can assure you, that will not be Lord Pembroke."

Miss Caroline took a small biscuit from a tray on the table in front of them. "It sounds as though your mother has other ideas."

"Yes, I know. I do wish she would stop pushing me to marry. Due to Papa's declining health, and then his death, I started late, so I've only had one Season. Is it so terrible for me to not take the first man who offers marriage?"

"Pembroke is the third man you have turned down, young lady." Lady Melrose swept into the drawing room, a frown marring her still-lovely complexion. A frown Arabella had noticed was, of late, a perpetual expression for her once-carefree mother.

Since Arabella was an only child, the family estate had passed into the hands of a distant relative who was currently conducting business in India. They had been told by their solicitor the new Earl of Melrose was expected to return to England and take up residency in the fall.

Unfortunately, Arabella's late father had enjoyed a predilection for whiskey and faro, and a total lack of interest in the preservation of his estate. Mother had impressed upon Arabella several times that once her dowry was paid, there would be no funds left for her support, so unless her daughter took her in, she would have nowhere to live.

Via their solicitor, the new earl had offered to allow Lady Melrose to continue living at the estate, but her mother had turned up her nose at that offer. *She would live with her newly married daughter, she'd sniffed.*

"I've hardly turned down three ideal offers, Mother. Lord Pembroke never got the words out, and Mr. Featherington and Baron Smythe are both old enough to be my grandfather."

"Which is to your advantage, miss. They are both wealthy men and will die soon."

At Arabella's indrawn breath, her mother waved her hand. "No need for hysterics, young lady. It is a fact that both men were looking for a wife in order to have an heir before they cocked up their toes."

And I do not wish to be someone's broodmare.

If she said that out loud her mother would most definitely swoon, and a half hour would pass trying to restore her sensibilities. Instead, Arabella waved at the teapot. "Would you care for some tea, Mother?"

Lady Elizabeth and Miss Caroline had pretended they hadn't heard the exchange by softly mumbling to each other. But Arabella had no doubt they took in every word and would soon use it as fodder for their next morning call. Honestly, why couldn't Mother be a bit more circumspect?

"No tea, thank you, daughter. I am off to the milliner's. I will see you at dinner before we depart for the Ashbourne ball."

Arabella groaned inwardly at the reminder. At present, one of Arabella's animal patients was in dire need of supervision while it recovered from its injuries. The last time she had left one of the downstairs maids in charge of a patient, the poor thing had died.

Mother thought her concern for animals, and her desire to nurture them back to health, a nasty hobby. On the other hand, Arabella saw it as a way of keeping her brain from melting with all the talk of ribbons, gowns, gossip, and other nonsense most of the *ton* ladies lived for.

She'd already heard whispers at various events about her passion for animals and how unseemly it was for a young lady to delve into such goings-on. She sighed. Another reason she so disliked attending these functions.

Later that afternoon, Arabella entered the spare bedchamber where she kept the various animals under her care. The scant sunlight coming through the west window cast a soft glow over three dogs, one bird, and two cats. All had been injured in some way. She had been rescuing and treating animals since she was a young girl. Over Mother's objections, Arabella continued to not only bring home injured animals, but accept those poor creatures who appeared at the back door of their townhouse. Despite the whisperings at social events, word of her healing skills had spread throughout London, and those unable to care for their injured pets brought them to her.

She could not remember a time when she did not love caring for animals. As a young girl, more comfortable with the family's groom than other girls of her class, she'd spent time learning about horses and their care. That knowledge had driven her to various books on veterinary practices, and then eventually to helping other injured animals.

"Well, look at you, Miss Aphrodite. You appear well today." She addressed the large white long-haired cat which ran her pink tongue over her fur. The animal continued her ministrations, ignoring Arabella. Something she did on a regular basis. The gash on the left side of her body was slowly healing. Arabella had sewn her up, and did her best to keep the cat from licking the wound.

Arabella would bring the cat to the elderly Lady Oswald, who had agreed to take Miss Aphrodite when Arabella had mentioned her to the ladies at her morning calls. Arabella placed the basket on the floor and carefully lifted the cat and placed her inside. "I know you will just love your new home. Lady Oswald is quite anxious to have your company."

Since it was a pleasant day, Arabella and her maid, Sophia, elected to walk through the park to reach Lady Oswald's house. The air was unseasonably warm, and the soft breeze tickled the hair that had escaped her bonnet, blowing the wisps into her eyes. The blanket over the top of the basket where Miss Aphrodite rested began to shift. "I believe our passenger has awakened from her nap."

Lifting the blanket, Arabella stared down at the animal, who stared right back at her. Before she could even say a word, the cat jumped from the basket and raced away.

"Miss Aphrodite, come back!" Arabella handed the basket to Sophia then picked up her skirts and, abandoning all dignity, dashed after the cat. "Come back," she yelled, ignoring the people around her who turned to gawk in her direction.

The cat tore over the ground, apparently chasing a small rodent. Arabella placed her hand on her bonnet, which threatened to sail from her head. The cat continued on, and Arabella was beginning to get a stitch in her side when a young gentleman headed toward her from the other direction. Right in Miss Aphrodite's path. "My lord, can you please catch my cat?"

Apparently deep in thought as he enjoyed a stroll, the man looked up just as the rodent ran up his leg. Miss Aphrodite hurled herself at his chest, the weight of her body knocking him backward into a tree. Waving his hands to avoid the mouse and the cat, he slammed into the trunk, slid down, and landed in a puddle of muddy water. His hat flew off, and Miss Aphrodite jumped from his shoulder onto the tree, scaling the branches, disappearing from sight.

• • •

Nash, the Earl of Clarendon, stared stupidly at the woman who raced up to him, holding her side and panting. "I'm so sorry, my lord. Are you well?"

"Lady Arabella?" With his legs stretched out, he shook his head, trying to clear it, and stared up at her. He remembered her from a few social events they'd attended together. If his memory was correct, she was a friend of his sister, Eugenia, Marchioness of Devon.

"Yes. Oh my goodness, Lord Clarendon. I am so very sorry." Her face was flushed, her bonnet askew, her eyes—for lack of a better word—wild. That look, however, did not detract from the girl's visage. Lady Arabella was, indeed, a very attractive young lady. Not that this was the time to dwell on such a thing.

He placed his hand on the soft, muddy ground and jumped up. The back of his breeches clung to him in such a way that he knew they were mud filled. As was his glove, he noticed with chagrin. "What happened?"

"My cat." She continued to pant and barely got the words out.

"Your cat?"

"Yes. She got out of my basket." She pointed behind her to where a woman, obviously a maid, hurried up, carrying a basket with a blanket draped over it. Lady Arabella looked behind him, up at the branches of the tree. "Oh dear. She's climbed up, and now she can't come down."

Just as she uttered the words, a loud howl came from above. The devil take it, was the animal now going to drop on his head?

Lady Arabella glanced frantically from the top of the tree to him. "My lord, can I ask a favor of you?"

Still trying to process everything that had just happened, he looked at her for a minute before answering. "A favor?"

"Yes, please. Can you climb the tree and rescue my cat?" She chewed her lower lip, which would have appealed to him if he wasn't standing in wet, muddy breeches, with an animal yowling over his head.

"Climb the tree?" Surely the woman was daft. This was Hyde Park, for heaven's sake, not his country estate where he'd done such things as a lad. "I am sorry, my lady, but I fear I am not dressed for tree climbing. Animals are most adept at rescuing themselves."

She waved at the animal howling above his head. "What sort of a gentleman are you? You would walk off and leave that poor animal in distress?" Her voice rose on the last few words.

Nash glanced around at the two couples who strolled nearby, who were watching the exchange with a bit too much interest and humor. The last thing he wanted was to draw more attention to himself.

"Please?" Apparently, she felt a change of tactics would work better. Her irresistible hazel eyes filled with tears, and her plump lower lip quivered. Bloody, bloody hell. The one thing he could not countenance was a woman's tears. He ran his hand down his face before he remembered his glove was muddy.

She winced.

"I just smeared mud all over my face, did I not?"

She nodded and continued to chew her lip. At least she had the good sense not to laugh, as he was sure she was wont to do. The cat continued to screech, and to his horror, a crowd was gathering. "Very well." He stripped off the muddy gloves, then his coat. The sooner he got the blasted animal out of the tree and back into its basket, the sooner he could go home, have a bath, and down a very large glass of brandy.

"Oh, thank you so much." She stood, wringing her hands.

"Yes, well. Let's have at it." He grabbed a low-lying branch above his head and swung himself up. He balanced on the branch and reached, but was not high enough to grab the irritating cat.

"Miss Aphrodite, come down, please. Let this nice gentleman help you."

Nash looked down, his eyes wide. "Miss Aphrodite?"

"Yes. That's her name."

Miss Aphrodite.

"If you call her by her name she might warm up to you and come down," she shouted up at him.

He was already making a spectacle of himself in the tree, his arse covered in mud, and dried, caked dirt on his face. He would damn well not call the animal by that ridiculous moniker. "Come here, kitty."

That sounded no better. The cat wailed and looked down at him. He grabbed another branch and moved higher. Reaching out, he almost had her when she hissed and leaped right at him, her nails clinging to his waistcoat. "Ouch!"

He grabbed the animal by its back fur just as a loud sneeze erupted from his nose. Nash wrapped his arm around the branch next to him as he sneezed several more times.

"Oh my lord. Are you allergic to cats?"

He looked down at Lady Arabella. "I've never been this close to one before, so apparently, I am, my lady." He began his descent, trying to hang on to the hissing, scratching cat. More sneezes. "I will drop the animal, if you can catch it."

"Oh no, my lord. She will just run off again."

Bloody hell. The best thing that could happen to any of them was to have the blasted cat run off. As far away from him as possible. He continued to hang on to the feline until he jumped to the ground. He heard the sound of fabric tearing as his feet landed. Nash closed his eyes and groaned when he realized the back of his breeches had just split.

With a scowl, he turned the cat over to Lady Arabella, who purred and talked nonsense to the devil-feline. She tucked the creature into the basket and covered it with the cloth once more.

"I suggest you remove that animal before it runs off again." He took out a handkerchief and attempted to brush some of the dried dirt from his face.

"How can I possibly thank you, my lord?" Lady Arabella's face shone with happiness as she tucked the blanket snugly around the basket. The animal did not move, seemingly worn out from its adventure.

"You can thank me by never allowing that—thing—out of the house again." He sneezed once more and wiped his nose. He retrieved his coat from the grass and shrugged into it, hoping it covered enough of his breeches to allow him a dignified retreat from the park. "Now, I will bid you good day, Lady Arabella." He bowed as if he wasn't covered in mud, with a tear in his breeches, and his face dirty. Turning on his heel, he strode out of the park and toward his townhouse.

• • •

Later that evening, Nash descended the stairs to the Ashbourne ballroom to join his sister, Eugenia, and her husband, Lord Devon. He squashed the urge to turn tail and run when he noticed Lady Arabella standing next to Eugenia, chatting away. Just watching her, he felt a sneeze coming on. She certainly looked a lot better than she had the last time he'd seen her. Of course, he imagined he looked more restored, as well.

Earlier, his valet, Andrews, had sniffed his disapproval at the condition in which Nash had returned home. With raised eyebrows, but no comment—none was necessary— he had helped Nash out of his clothes and, holding them by his fingertips, marched across the room to drop them into a bundle on the floor. "A bath, my lord?"

"Yes. But a large glass of brandy first."

"Indeed."

Pushing the scene from his mind, he stepped up to the group. "Good evening, Lady Arabella, Eugenia, Devon."

"Oh, Lord Clarendon." Arabella extended her hand. "Thank you once again for rescuing my cat. Well, actually, she really wasn't my cat—"

"Excuse me?" Had he suffered indignities and angered his valet for naught? "Not your cat?"

"Yes. You see, I was delivering the cat to Lady Oswald when Miss Aphrodite escaped."

"Then it was Lady Oswald's cat?"

"Well, yes, sort of."

He knew he should just drop the subject, but Eugenia and Devon eyed him with curiosity, so he felt the—foolish—need to ask, "Would you care to explain, my lady?"

"I rescued Miss Aphrodite from an alley on Oxford Street after a very bad cat fight. I sewed up her injuries and took care of her until she healed. Lady Oswald expressed a desire to own a cat, so I offered her Miss Aphrodite. I was delivering her when she ran off this afternoon."

"You rescued Lady Arabella's cat, Nash? How very sweet." Eugenia smiled at him in such a way he felt ridiculous. No one had ever called him sweet before. Nor would anyone ever again, if he had anything to say about it.

He'd gotten disgustingly muddy, torn his breeches,

suffered from sneezing fits—all to rescue a cat that probably belonged in the wild anyway. Anxious to turn the conversation, he extended his hand to Eugenia. "May I have the privilege of this dance, sister?" The orchestra was just starting up a cotillion, and he wished to be gone from Lady Arabella's company before he hurled insults at her and her animal.

"No. This baby is giving me a bit of stomach upset." She placed her hand on her tummy. "I'd heard morning time was the problem, and although I have some difficulties with my breakfast, lately evening seems just as troublesome. We will be leaving shortly."

"After a good night's rest, we are off to the country early tomorrow morning." A sly grin crossed Devon's face, and he bent down to whisper in Eugenia's ear. She drew in a sharp breath, and a deep shade of red rose to her cheeks.

Nash groaned, not wanting to know what his brother-in-law had said. "All right, you two. Devon, remember, Eugenia is my baby sister. I do not wish to know what it was you whispered to her, but please discontinue before I feel the need to ask you to step outside."

A wide grin split his brother-in-law's face. "She's my wife!"

"And my sister!"

"Enough!" Eugenia laughed and placed her hand on Nash's chest. "All is fine. I promise." She fanned herself and cast a sideways glance at her husband, who studied her with a look which Nash preferred not to be aware.

Deciding he had had enough of their infatuation with each other, he bowed and kissed Eugenia's cheek. "I shall leave the two of you to toddle on home. 'Tis difficult for me to stand here while smothered with all this love floating around. Have a safe journey tomorrow."

Lady Arabella looked back and forth between Lord Clarendon and Lady Devon. "I believe felicitations are in order?"

"Yes." Eugenia smiled. "We are expecting an heir in several months." She turned to Nash. "Since we are leaving, I am sure Lady Arabella would be delighted to join you in this dance, brother."

He groaned inwardly. Hell and damnation. He'd been trying to get away from the chit. Only disaster could loom on the horizon when this woman was involved. But, drawing on his manners, he bowed. "Lady Arabella, would you honor me with this dance?"

Chapter Two

Arabella placed her hand in Clarendon's as he led her to the dance floor. He had looked about as pleased to be forced to dance with her as she was with him. Besides still being embarrassed at the trouble she'd caused him earlier in the day, she had the distinct impression he disapproved of her, and her animals.

"You don't like me very much, do you?" Never one for evading an issue, she went right to the crux of the matter. He might as well admit it so they could get this dance over with and go their separate ways.

He viewed her with that arrogant raised eyebrow of his she'd noticed in the park. "Most likely about as much as you like me."

Shaking his head, he pinched the bridge of his nose. "Actually, I apologize, Lady Arabella. That is not true. I don't know you well enough to dislike you. What I have an aversion to is rescuing animals in public. Then again, perhaps 'tis best if we pretend to enjoy the dance, thus avoiding another scene similar to the one you caused in the park with your odd habits."

Well, then.

A scene, indeed. He had absolutely no say in how she conducted her life. If she wished to rescue scores of animals and treat them for injures and ailments, it was none of his business. She cast him a glance from under lowered eyelashes. It was too bad a man who looked so good had to be so difficult.

Clarendon's dark blond, curly hair hung a bit more over the back of his cravat than was fashionable, but it suited him well. It appeared his valet had attempted to tame the curls, but a few stubborn locks had sprung free and brushed his broad forehead. An aristocratic nose and full lips left no doubt he was descended from generations of nobility. His crystal blue eyes bore into her as he released her hand when they joined the line. They stood across from each other as the music began. He bowed, she curtsied, and they came together. She would be the bigger of them and clear the air. "I do wish to apologize for the trouble I caused you today, my lord."

They switched places. "'Tis nothing, I assure you." He extended his hand, and they moved together with the other dancers for a few steps.

"I disagree, my lord. You ended up muddy, with your clothes torn."

His jaw flexed as they moved around each other and joined the line of dancers again. "Of course, you disagree, but I assure you, my lady, 'twas nothing."

As they weaved in and out of the other dancers, she mumbled, "What do you mean 'of course I disagree,' and why cannot you accept an apology freely given? Are you always so disagreeable, then?"

They joined hands once more. "Perhaps because I do not wish to be reminded of the incident."

Separating, they moved around each other, dipping with the music. "I believe you are merely being stubborn."

Nash closed his eyes. "And I believe *you* are being stubborn."

"I am not being stubborn. I simply want to extend my apologies for the mishap this afternoon."

They joined hands again and moved in a circle. "Fine. Your apology is accepted."

Another couple switched places with them, eyeing them with curiosity. "There, now. Was that so very hard?"

"My dear lady, do you wish to dance, or converse?"

They stepped forward, hand in hand, to the head of the line. "Can we not do both?"

"Perhaps I lose count if I talk and dance."

Her eyebrows rose and she offered a tight grin. "Cannot do two things at once, my lord? Is that why you had such a difficult time rescuing a poor cat?"

Nash came to an abrupt halt, causing the couple behind them to stumble. "I did not have a difficult time of it." He bent close to her ear and murmured. "Furthermore, I am finished with this conversation."

Arabella sniffed, but kept her mouth closed the rest of the dance. Far be it from her to wish to speak with the dreadful man. Even though the Earl of Clarendon was a darling of the *ton*, with numerous debutantes forever dropping handkerchiefs in his path, and most of the marriage-minded mamas' eyes on him, she found him arrogant and insufferable.

Despite their silence, they continued to glower at each other for the duration of the dance. Once the music ended, she curtsied, he bowed, and they went their separate ways.

Oh, the man could make a saint swear! All she had wanted to do was offer her apology. But could he graciously accept? No, he could not. The stubborn man had to make an issue of it.

Arabella sighed and studied the crowd. She had no idea where her mother had gone. Ordinarily, the woman never left her side. Across the room, she spotted Miss Caroline and Lady Elizabeth, heads together, chatting. She made her way through the throng to join them.

She'd only gone a few steps when she heard a dreaded voice behind her. "Lady Arabella." She turned to see Lord Pembroke pushing people aside, hurrying in her direction. Groaning inwardly, she glanced around for an escape. Unfortunately, with the amount of people crowding the area, there was virtually nowhere to go.

He caught up to her and reached for her hand. She allowed him to kiss it, thankful for her glove. "I would be honored to accompany you to the garden for a stroll. There is an important matter I wish to discuss with you."

The last thing she wanted to do was take a stroll in the garden with Lord Sausage Fingers. And she knew precisely what important matter to which he referred. Before she had a chance to refuse, the orchestra started up again. "Oh dear me, my lord, it appears my next partner is searching for me."

He turned to where she looked over his shoulder, and the only person facing them was the elderly Lord Graymore, who hadn't danced in decades. In fact, the poor man looked around as if he wasn't altogether sure where he was. Pembroke turned back. "I believe Graymore overestimated his abilities, if he requested this dance." He looked over his shoulder again at the elderly man who wandered in a different direction. "In fact, it appears he has even forgotten."

Arabella groaned. So much for subterfuge.

Pembroke held out his hand. "But not to disappoint a lady, I will be happy to partner you."

Good manners prohibited her from stamping her foot and shouting, *No, leave me alone*. Instead, she took his hand, grateful the number starting up was not a waltz. "I would be delighted, my lord."

The dance seemed to never end, and by the time it was

finished she was heated and desperately needed refreshment. "My lord, may I trouble you for a glass of lemonade? I find myself quite parched."

"Of course, my lady. It will be no trouble at all. I shall be right back." Pembroke turned from her with a slight bow and made his way through the crowd, his bright-red hair visible as he wended his way to the refreshment table.

Arabella sighed as she watched him go. She should probably permit the man to propose so she could turn him down and allow his dignity to be restored. What she disliked more than anything was the constant pressure she felt from Mother to choose a husband. She knew it was her duty, and really did want to make sure she and her mother were not out on the street, but the new Earl of Melrose did not seem to be in a hurry to remove them from the premises.

She looked around the crowded room. As most balls went, the Ashbourne event could be considered a crush. Too many bodies forced into a space not large enough for them all, with feathers dangling from women's hair, poking gentlemen in the eye. Strong perfumes and hair pomades mingled with the scent of overheated bodies.

Suddenly feeling anxious and unable to breathe, Arabella forgot about her drink and stumbled her way through the crowd, heading to the ladies retiring room. Crowds always bothered her, especially Polite Society crowds. If she had her way, she would avoid the Season at all costs and retire to the country to take care of animals and live her life the way she chose.

Unfortunately, for a young woman with a mother to think of, and no resources of her own, marriage was inevitable, and the Season was where one secured one's future.

The bedchamber set aside for the benefit of the female guests was a haven of peace and quiet. Two ladies conversed as they sat at the dressing tables while a maid tended to them.

Arabella drew in a deep breath and immediately felt better. She would relax even more if she could free herself of her stays, but that would not happen for hours yet.

Women came and went, but few acknowledged her presence. She was certainly not one of the *ton's* favorite young ladies. Her propensity to find and treat injured and sick animals had given rise to whispered gossip that she delved into unladylike behavior. That, perhaps, might be the reason she'd only received the attentions of men of a great age. Desperate for an heir, any young chit would do.

Nevertheless, a peaceful ten minutes went by as she applied a cold cloth to her head and rested on the settee, watching the ladies fuss and run the maid ragged with demands. Feeling refreshed, she stood and shook out her skirts. What she would prefer was to find Mother and return home. Without a doubt, Lord Pembroke would still be on the prowl for her, and she did not want to deal with him tonight.

As she descended the steps to the ballroom, Miss Hayward, a long-time friend, waved at her.

"Lady Arabella!" She clutched a piece of paper in her hand. The girl managed to squeeze past two matrons whispering behind their fans, their eyes cast at a young girl flirting with two men. No doubt the girl would be classified as "fast" by morning.

"Good evening, Cynthia, I haven't seen you in a while."

The young lady joined her, a smile on her rounded face. "I know. I think we have managed to attend different affairs so far this Season." She gave Arabella a hug, and they kissed the air near each other's cheeks.

"Before I forget why I sought you out, your mother asked me to deliver this note to you."

Arabella frowned and took the paper from the girl's hand. How unusual for her mother to send a note. "Is she well? Did she appear distressed when she gave you this?"

"No." Cynthia shook her head, her blond curls dancing alongside her face. "She appeared a bit flushed, but I think it was more from the heat of the room than anything untoward."

Arabella opened the paper, a frown pulling her brows together.

A situation has arisen that requires your presence in the Ashbourne's library. A footman will direct you.

. . .

Nash accepted a glass of champagne from a footman and once again scanned the crowd, searching for Lady Grace and her mother. He had been considering making her an offer for a while now and saw no reason to continue the delay. If the opportunity presented itself, he would speak with her this evening and visit with her guardian in the morning to work out the marriage settlements.

He and Lady Grace had gone on carriage rides, attended the theater, and danced no more than one dance at each *ton* affair over the last Season and the course of this Season thus far. Twice, he had arrived at her house during calling hours, and after observing her with her guests, he was certain she would make an acceptable wife.

Although quite young—barely eighteen years—she was a charming young lady who had been raised to be a nobleman's wife. Truth be known, the girl was a bit on the silly side, as most young girls tended to be, but with his guidance, she would mature nicely into the perfect countess. She had seemed amenable to his attentions, and no doubt expected an offer to be forthcoming. At least her mother certainly did, and while she was too refined to come right out and ask, he knew her marriage-minded mama was waiting with bated breath.

Every time he had come close to actually asking for

her hand, however, something had held him back. But this nonsense had to end. He needed a wife, and the time seemed right. He'd done all the things a young gentleman of the *ton* did after University: drinking, gaming, visiting opera dancers, and now he was ready to settle down and see to filling his nursery.

While he would never feel the passionate love for Lady Grace he saw between Eugenia and Devon, there was no doubt he held Lady Grace in great regard. In his opinion, that was the only requirement for a successful marriage. Eventually, as the years passed and they raised children, a strong affection would grow between them.

Her generous dowry — should the rumors prove correct — was very appealing, as well. He hated to think about that part of it, but there you have it. His estate was in serious need of an infusion of blunt, or they would be in deep trouble. When his father had passed a few years ago, the situation had been concerning, but nowhere near as dire. It seemed no matter how well the tenants did, Mr. Bowers, his man of business, reported they were still low on funds. Once he got the matter settled with Lady Grace, he would have to make a trip to Suffolk to see if he could get an idea of what was going wrong.

"You seem to be spending a great deal of time watching the staircase, Nash. Are you perhaps looking for a particular young lady?" Lord Mullens grinned in his direction as he took a sip of champagne.

Switching his attention from the staircase to Mullens, he said, "I believe the time has come for me to select a bride."

"And you've decided to take whatever female comes down the stairs next?" Mullens regarded him with the famous crooked grin that made ladies melt at his feet. "I am amazed that with all the young ladies — and their mamas — casting invitations in your direction you have avoided the parson's noose for so long."

"Leave off, Mullens. There is a particular woman, but for now, I shall keep her name to myself."

"Rumor has it that Lady Grace will be the next Countess of Clarendon."

Drat! He hated how these things got started. Preferring to keep his business to himself, Nash was never the type who bandied his affairs about. "Whomever I offer for will be the first to know, not the rest of the *ton*, regardless of their hunger for the next *on dit*."

"Ah, sounds as though the man is besotted and fears someone snatching up his lady love before he has a chance to speak his piece."

"Is not there someone else you can plague, Mullens? I'm sure there are several ladies here tonight who would enjoy your attention. I, on the other hand, do not, so I will leave you to your conquests." Nash strolled away, wishing Lady Grace would appear. She'd assured him at his last afternoon call that she and her mother would be attending.

His lady love, indeed. He was selecting a bride, not a mistress. Love was for besotted fools like Devon, not him. Although he did not intend to maintain a mistress once wed, he still preferred a marriage of respect and affection. Once love entered into it, emotions ran rampant and things got messy.

If anything proved that point, all he had to do was remember Lord Wentworth, whom he'd gone to University with. The poor sap had fallen madly in love with Lady Maryann Wesley, and had pursued the woman until she accepted his offer. Within months of their wedding, she had taken a lover, and Wentworth had continued to make a fool of himself before the *ton*.

The entire debacle had ended in disgrace when he took a gun to his head. No. No love and volatile emotions for him. A good, solid marriage with no romantic entanglements was all he needed.

He rubbed his head as he proceeded to the refreshment table for a lemonade.

He'd been fighting a headache since his encounter with Lady Arabella's cat that afternoon. As the hours passed, his head had hurt more and more, and the glass of champagne had made it worse. This was one of those headaches that would only go away with quiet and sleep.

Since he and Ashbourne's middle son had been friends at Eton, Nash had spent time at the family's townhouse and he was familiar with the layout. He would retire to the library for ten or fifteen minutes and surely by then, Lady Grace would have arrived. He would have a dance with her, take her to the garden, offer his proposal, and then leave for home.

Nash exited the ballroom through the French doors. He went down the patio steps and turned right, following the path to another set of steps that reached the French doors leading to Lady Ashbourne's sitting room. He carefully crossed the room in the darkness and exited, accessing the corridor. Candles burning in sconces along the walls cast a dim light, but enough for him to make his way several doors down and enter the library. Once the heavy wooden door closed, noise from the ballroom receded, and peace descended on him like a welcoming shroud.

The smell of the books greeted him, reminding him of his own library. The one in town was adequate but his library in Suffolk was immense, and he'd spent many a day there, reading all the books his father, and the Lords Clarendon before him, had amassed.

He strolled to the window and looked out at the darkness. Gas lights flickered along the winding garden path, illuminating Lady Ashbourne's spring flower gardens. He turned when the sound of the door opening drew his attention.

A young woman entered. From the dim light he could

barely make out her countenance. As she walked farther into the room, the moonlight from the window caught her and he sucked in a surprised breath.

Lady Arabella.

Bloody hell. What the devil was *she* doing here? Finding another way to torment him?

She closed the door behind her and moved forward. "I am sorry to disturb you, my lord but I received a note to meet my mother here."

"Ah, perhaps she has more animals for you to rescue?" He raised one eyebrow, delighting in the look of annoyance on her face. Why he enjoyed irritating her was a puzzle. But he did like to watch her lips tighten and her cheeks flush a lovely red. Although she pretended to be a lady, there was a lot of fire and passion in the young woman.

Lady Arabella drew herself up. "I do not know why she wanted to meet me. In fact, the entire thing seems suspicious, now that I think about it." She waved a paper in his face. "Did you write this note?"

"What?" He reared back. "Why in heaven's name would I ask you, of all people, to meet me here? Mayhaps you saw me enter and want me to climb the library selves to rescue another creature?"

"Oh, you." She stamped her foot. "I almost wish I had left Miss Aphrodite in the tree rather than ask anything of you."

"I, too, wish you had decided on that course of action. Then I would have been able to enjoy my stroll in the park."

They glared at each other. "Well, I see no reason to stay here. I must have misunderstood her note." She sniffed. "I am sorry to have caused you any bother, my lord."

Chagrined at appearing to be an ogre, he said, "Are you able to find your way back to the door? It is quite dark in here."

"I shall be fine. Thank you." She turned her back to him

and moved only a few steps when she stumbled. Always the gentleman, Nash rushed forward and caught her in his arms just as she would have fallen to the floor.

The door to the library flew open and several people stood at the entrance. "What is the meaning of this?" Her chin raised, a woman stormed into the room, a contingent of cohorts right behind her.

"Bloody hell," Nash mumbled as he stood before the crowd, in a darkened room, with Lady Arabella Danvers in his arms.

Chapter Three

Black dots danced before Arabella's eyes right before she shook her head, refusing to allow herself the luxury of swooning. She had no idea what was going on, but knew she needed her full faculties to avoid the pending disaster.

"Mother!" She moved away from Lord Clarendon and took a few steps. She raised her fingertips to her forehead, as once again, dizziness overcame her. A strong arm wrapped around her waist, keeping her from tumbling to the floor. "I received a note—"

"Say no more!" Her mother raised her hand in the air. She turned to Lord Clarendon. "My lord, unhand my daughter."

"I would be most happy to accommodate your request, madam, but if I do so, I can guarantee she will slip to the floor." Arabella felt his voice vibrate right through their clothing. His scent of sandalwood drifted to her where their bodies touched. With his arm still around her waist, he led her to the settee. She sat, still confused as to what was going on. Clarendon remained standing, his feet apart, hands loosely fisted at his side, facing the crowd.

He glanced at her and bent to whisper into her ear. "Perhaps you should lower your head, my lady."

"Do not whisper in my daughter's ear." Mother's eyes snapped.

Arabella tried to make sense out of what was happening. Mother was supposed to meet her here, which she did, but only after she'd been caught with Lord Clarendon. Was he supposed to be here as well? Had Mother done something to arrange all of this? But why Lord Clarendon, of all people? As far as Mother knew, they were barely acquainted.

Lord Ashbourne made his way through the crowd and circled the room, lighting candles and bringing into focus what Arabella desperately wished to block from her vision. Mother stood at the forefront, with Ladies Beauchamp and Dickinson, along with Mrs. Humphries, next to her. They all stared at her and Lord Clarendon in horror.

Another woman and a young girl joined them. The two came into view and Arabella let out a groan, wishing it were possible to close off one's ears.

"My lord!" A wail erupted from Lady Grace. Her hand covered her mouth while she took in the scene. Closing her eyes, Lady Grace leaned her head on her mother's shoulder. Lord Clarendon mumbled to himself, but Arabella didn't hear the comment. However, given the rumors of the expectations Lady Grace had where Lord Clarendon was concerned, he'd probably uttered words she did not want to hear.

Lady Grace's mother speared Clarendon with a look that Arabella was most grateful hadn't been cast in her direction.

Then it was.

She gulped.

"Lady Melrose, I received a note—" A nasally voice joined the group.

Mother spun on her heel and faced Lord Pembroke, who was breathing heavily and wiping the sweat from his forehead while he pushed his way through the crowd. "I wasn't sure which room was the library—"

"Not now, my lord," she said through gritted teeth.

Lord Pembroke? Mother had sent notes to both her and Lord Pembroke? Most likely to have *them* caught in a compromising situation. She never would have thought Mother would do such a thing, but there seemed no other explanation for the events that had just taken place.

Except Clarendon had been here—for whatever reason— and now this was a mess, and she was ruined.

"Since this is my library, can someone please explain to me what is going on?" Lord Ashbourne glared in Clarendon's direction.

Clarendon looked down at Arabella as she watched him. Visions of her life as a ruined woman, with nowhere to go to avoid censure and no hope of the life she'd always dreamed of, flashed in her mind. She and Mother would have no home, and the disgrace would most likely send the woman into a decline.

She held her breath as he continued to study her. A slight kernel of absolute terror settled in her stomach. Certainly, the man would not make this situation worse by offering for her? There must be other, more palatable solutions to this catastrophe. They just needed to keep their heads and think it through.

Seeming to reach a decision, he extended his hand. Not knowing what he was up to, but hoping he had a way to get them out of this without creating a disaster, she reached for his hand and stood on shaky legs. Her heart pounded so hard she swore they heard it out in the ballroom. She was aware of the stillness of the guests who watched them, and the whimpering of Lady Grace.

His lordship continued to stare at her as he took her other hand in his and spoke, "I apologize to all of you for the interruption in your evening's entertainment. I believe you have found us just as Lady Arabella made me the happiest of men by accepting my offer of marriage."

Lady Grace wailed and tumbled to the floor. The blackness Arabella had been fighting finally took control, and with a soft sigh she slumped against her newly betrothed's body.

. . .

Nash looked aghast at the two women. One lying on the floor at her mother's feet, the other in his arms. Since he'd already offered for Lady Arabella in order to avoid her ruination, he bent, and sliding his hands under her knees, picked her up.

She was light as a feather, and the simple scent of lemons and lavender drifted from her. Her soft curves nestled against his body, but all he wanted to do was drop her on the nearest settee and run for his life. The marriage he had planned with Lady Grace—whose mother was reviving her by waving a vinaigrette under her nose—was no longer to be.

Damn it all to hell! Here he'd been, moments away from offering for Lady Grace, and now he found himself betrothed to Lady Arabella, of all people! A woman who rescued cats! Cats! He would be sneezing for the rest of his life.

Unless he was arguing with her.

Based on the look of longing on Pembroke's face, Lady Melrose had set this up for him. He couldn't help but wonder if Arabella had been involved as well, although given her response thus far, it was unlikely she'd been a part of the scheme.

No doubt Pembroke had been the desired target of Lady Melrose's ploy. The man looked dumbfounded at Lady Arabella, disappointment plainly written on his fleshy, sweating face. Nash surmised the man had been the mother's choice, but given the setup, Pembroke had apparently not been Lady Arabella's choice. Then, again, *he* hadn't been her choice, either. Nevertheless, now they were engaged.

He laid her on the settee and tapped her gently on her cheek.

"It appears there is nothing further to deal with tonight," Lord Ashbourne spoke with authority as he began to usher the crowd from the room.

"I will not leave my defenseless, unconscious daughter here with this man." Lady Melrose sniffed.

Just then Lady Arabella began to move and her eyelids fluttered open. She took a look around the room and with a slight moan, closed her eyes again.

"Madam, your daughter is now in the hands of her betrothed. I suggest we all leave and allow her to recover." Ashbourne studied Nash. "I assume you are prepared to meet with Lady Melrose's representatives in the morning?"

"Yes. Of course." Nash turned to Lady Melrose. "With whom must I speak?" Nash knew Lord Melrose had passed some time ago. Rumor had it that his heir was out of the country and would soon be taking up residence at the Melrose estate.

"Since there is no guardian, you may contact my solicitors." She eyed her daughter, who was attempting to gain her feet. "I will send for my carriage so I can take her home."

Nash took Lady Arabella's arm and steadied her as she stood. "No, my lady. I would prefer to accompany my *betrothed* home." He gritted his teeth at those words, cursing his upbringing that refused to allow him to be part of a woman's ruination. "I will send for my carriage."

"But—" Lady Melrose looked alarmed. Did she believe he would actually harm Lady Arabella? But then, how well did she know him? Still very much annoyed at the woman's machinations, he felt a need to punish her a bit.

"You may return in your carriage, madam. I will see Lady Arabella home." His voice gave no quarter.

The woman blew out a deep breath of air. "As you wish, my lord." She turned, and giving Lady Arabella one last glance, left the room.

As the last of the witnesses passed thorough the doorway, Lord Ashbourne followed them. He stopped for a moment and studied Nash and Lady Arabella. "I have no idea what went on here tonight, but I commend you for doing the right thing, young man. I have a feeling you are as befuddled as I am."

Nash gave his host a slight bow. "Thank you, sir. Would you be so kind as to have my carriage brought around? I would like to give Lady Arabella a bit more time to compose herself."

"I will do that, but please leave the door open. We don't need things to get any worse than they are right now." Once he walked away, Nash turned to Lady Arabella, his voice lowered. "The only thing keeping me from wringing your neck is a slight belief that you had no part in the debacle this evening."

She shook her head furiously. "Absolutely not. I would never put myself in this positon on purpose. However, please be aware that your gallant overture will be for naught. I have no intention of marrying you."

He placed his hands on his hips and glared at her. "Excuse me? Do you think I wish to marry *you*? A woman who chases animals in public?"

She sniffed. "Good, then we are in agreement. We will go our separate ways, since I don't give a tinker's damn for Society's opinions." Lady Arabella licked her lips. Kissable lips, he noted for the first time. Soft, plump, and red. She continued, "'Tis an easy problem to solve. We can wait a while to keep all the gossip lovers happy, then I will cry off."

. . .

Arabella still felt a bit lightheaded, but she wanted more than anything to escape this horrid room and go home. Lock herself in her bedchamber and not emerge until she was as old as the Widow Johnson. What a mess this had become!

"You little fool." Lord Clarendon snapped. "Do you honestly believe crying off an engagement would restore your reputation? Especially after being caught in my arms in a dark room? By ourselves? Do you think it can get any worse than that? Well, it can. If you call off, your reputation will be in shreds."

Despite her flip words, she was no half-wit about Society's condemnation. But she had never wanted to have Polite Society dictate how she lived. However, she would not concede this point to him. "I don't care one whit about my reputation."

Another raised eyebrow. "Obviously not, given your behavior thus far."

"And what is that supposed to mean?"

"Do you truly wish to resume our discussion from before? Your behavior in the park was beyond the pale for a young lady. Racing around, your skirts hiked above your ankles, chasing a cat."

She pointed her finger at his chest. "This is precisely why I do not want you to rescue me by pretending we are engaged. You disapprove of me, I find you arrogant, and a marriage between us would likely lead to one of us swinging from the end of a rope."

As she stared into his surprised eyes, she had another thought. Had he planned an assignation with Lady Grace? An ill-timed meet-up that had gone awry by her own mother's maneuvers? "What were *you* doing in here, Clarendon?"

He raised his eyebrows. "I am suffering from the residue

of a megrim due to an encounter in the park this afternoon with a feline." Apparently pausing to allow that comment to take hold, he added, "I merely came in here to gather my thoughts and have a few minutes of peace and quiet. And we now know how that turned out." He crossed his arms over his chest. "What brought you here? Were you following me?"

"Following *you*? I can assure you I would have no reason to follow you anywhere." She held up the note Cynthia had handed her. "I received a note from my mother asking me to attend her here. It now appears to me she planned for Lord Pembroke to find me, alone, with perhaps the same ending in mind in which we now find ourselves."

"Had you wanted to marry Pembroke?"

Her head snapped back, and her eyes grew wide. "Lord, no."

For the first time all evening, Lord Clarendon smiled. Which, in turn, brought a smile to her face, as well.

"Come. It is time I escorted you home." He took her elbow and walked toward the door.

She stopped as they reached the portal. "No doubt everyone beyond that door will be leaping for joy at my supposed disgrace."

"Buck up, Lady Arabella," he whispered as he tightened his grip and moved her forward. "This is only the beginning."

With his words echoing in her ears, he escorted her out of the library, down the corridor, and to the front door. Whispers floated from behind cupped hands, eyes peered over the tops of fans, and knowing smirks covered the faces of many of the men.

Arabella had never been so embarrassed in her life. Although, due to her odd propensities, she'd never been a favorite of the *ton*, she had at least enjoyed a somewhat respectable reputation. Oftentimes she thought, were she not an earl's daughter, she would not be welcomed into some homes. After all, dignified ladies of the *ton* did not rescue animals.

Now her mother had placed her in a position that could very well take years to overcome. To say nothing of the fact that she found herself engaged to a man she barely knew, and didn't even like. Add to the mess that Lord Clarendon had been about to offer for another, and the entire matter was a catastrophe.

She was sure that once he had time to think it over, he would come to the sane realization that they should not marry each other.

He assisted her into her pelisse and then held her elbow as they made their way down the steps to his carriage. For the life of her, she couldn't understand why he was being so gracious when she was more than willing to give him a way out. Their encounters had left her with the firm belief that he was no happier with her than she was with him. Though she had some knowledge of him through her friendship with his sister, Eugenia, who was quite fond of her brother. And Eugenia found him tolerable. At least he was honorable—to a fault, it seemed.

He *had* been gentlemanly enough to rescue Miss Aphrodite…grudgingly. It was a far cry from rescuing her from her mother's machinations. Especially since it meant spending the rest of their lives together.

There was also the multitude of young ladies who would be crying into their often-dropped handkerchiefs now that Lord Clarendon was off the marriage mart. If she could not convince him to stop this foolishness, the darling of the *ton* would be her husband.

Her husband.

Oh lord, Mother, what have you done?

• • •

Nash handed Lady Arabella into his carriage and climbed in behind her. She huddled in the corner, facing the window. He took the opportunity to study her in the scant light. Certainly not difficult to look at, as he'd noted before. Of course, that was when she'd merely been a pest with odd habits and not his intended bride. She had an acceptable figure underneath her gown. A form he'd noticed even more so when he'd picked her up. Her warm, soft curves had fit nicely against him.

Her skin was creamy, her lips lush and full. He would certainly not find bedding her a chore. But there was more to marriage than a romp between the sheets. She had to be able to handle his household and maneuver them among Society—accepting and rejecting invitations. She needed to plan and preside over dinner parties, garden parties, and balls. One day she would have to guide their children from childhood to adulthood.

Although he knew very little of her, he assumed she'd been trained by her governesses and tutors in all the appropriate competencies. No doubt she played the pianoforte well, stitched a lovely needlepoint, and produced acceptable watercolors. She was probably fluid in French, and perhaps German. Much like he'd found Lady Grace to be.

But the animals. That would be a problem, especially since he could not be near a cat without a sneezing fit. Well, that was something she would have to leave behind. As well as her stubborn nature. Once they married, he would be the one to make the decisions for the both of them. After all, when he'd awoken this morning, he'd had no intention of proposing marriage to Lady Arabella. But, if he put aside their recent unpleasant encounters, she would probably do as well as Lady Grace in the role of his countess.

It startled him to realize the two women were interchangeable. He had no great love or passion for Lady Grace. She had seemed an acceptable bride. And, of course, there had been her dowry.

Which left him with the question of Lady Arabella's dowry, something he was sure to discover when he met with her solicitor. "Why is it you have no guardian?" The question popped out before he even thought about it.

A surprised Lady Arabella, no doubt deep in her own thoughts about the upcoming nuptials, faced him. "I had reached my majority when my papa passed last year."

"You are two and twenty, then?"

"Yes. Papa was ill for more than two years before his passing. We were unable to travel to Town. Then with the mourning period after he died, I was already a few years older than the other girls the year I came out." She raised her chin. "Do you have a problem with my age, my lord?"

God almighty, the girl seemed ready to begin an argument over anything he said.

"No. I was merely asking." He studied her. "Do you take offense at every comment?"

"It depends on who is making the comment. Most of yours seem to be insulting."

He sighed. "I meant no insult by asking why you have no guardian. However, I am finished with disagreements for the evening." He settled back in the carriage. Given Lady Arabella's age, that would explain why she seemed so sure of what she wanted and did not want. Unfortunately, she needed to realize that in the matter of their betrothal, they had no choice. In addition to her reputation, his would be tarnished, as well. A gentleman who was caught in a dark room, unchaperoned, with a young lady, was expected to step up and marry her. Whether that made sense or not was a moot point. It was the way of things in their world.

As the carriage rumbled through the streets of Mayfair, his thoughts wandered to Lady Grace. He'd planned on having to guide her into her new role as his wife. At eighteen years, she was young, and had shown signs of immaturity that he knew he'd have to deal with.

Truth be told, her constant chattering about nonsense had grated on his nerves more than once. On carriage rides and walks in the garden, he'd attempted to have more meaningful conversations with her. However, she had merely gazed at him with adoration and a bit of confusion. Hair ribbons, her wardrobe, hairstyles, and the latest gossip seemed to be their entire repartee when he was with her. Maybe having an older bride would suit him more.

That again left him with the odd, uncomfortable sense of the two women being transposable. An unnerving feeling, for sure. Had he not any attachment whatsoever to Lady Grace? Not that he'd intended to ever suffer the pangs of love and romance as Wentworth had, of course. Not for him the wrenching emotions of love that led to hurt feelings and messy botherations.

He focused his attention once more on Lady Arabella. "Since you did not wish to marry Pembroke, is there another you had hoped would offer?"

That was probably not a very gentlemanly question to ask, but nevertheless, he found he really wanted to know the answer. Would she be pining for someone else when he came to her bed?

"No, I have not been out in Society long enough to acquire a *tendre*."

He noted the sharpness of her voice. Was this a young lady who was not ready to accept the constraints of marriage? Hopefully, that would not cause him immense trouble. "I must admit surprise that a beautiful woman such as yourself has received no offers."

She turned and gave him a tight smile. "I did not say *no offers*. Merely that there was no one from whom I wished to receive an offer."

"Ah. So, there have been offers you've turned down?"

"Yes."

Now it made sense. Apparently, the young lady was being too particular, and her mama had decided to take matters into her own hands. "I take it Pembroke was the latest of your refusals?"

She nodded. "Although I never gave him the opportunity to actually propose." She shuddered. "I suppose, if things had gone the way Mother had planned, I would be faced with the dilemma of Pembroke's proposal." She turned to him, the earnestness of her words clearly written on her face. "I certainly don't desire love in my marriage, my lord, but I would like to be able to tolerate the man I marry."

"Indeed." His eyebrows rose. "And it seems I will now be that man." He leaned forward, gazing into her hazel eyes, made visible through the carriage lamp on the wall beside her head.

"So, tell me, Lady Arabella. Do you find me tolerable?"

Chapter Four

Arabella sucked in a breath as butterflies took up residence in her stomach at Clarendon's softly murmured words. Tolerable? Up to now she'd found him *barely* tolerable. To think she was expected to marry a man who disagreed with everything she said. But, she had found him to be a true gentleman. It would have been an easy thing for him to explain the truth of their encounter in the library, which would not have been believed by anyone.

Rumors about her virtue—or lack thereof—would have spread, looks would have been cast in her direction, and she would have been ruined.

He had saved her from all that by announcing their betrothal. The moment he had looked down at her when Lord Ashbourne had demanded to know what was going on in his library, her heart had sped up. She'd waited for him to blame her for stumbling into his peace and quiet, and then, quite literally, falling into his arms.

Lord Clarendon had done no such thing. He'd explained away their situation by relinquishing the woman he had planned to marry. But Arabella had no intention of allowing the situation to go as far as the altar.

However, something about the way he looked at her now made it seem as though all the air in the carriage had suddenly vanished. His heavy-lidded eyes were a much deeper color, and a slight twist to his lips gave him a rakish look. She wondered what it would feel like to have those lips covering hers. Calling herself so much a fool, she answered, "Yes, my lord. I find you tolerable." *Drat, how breathless I sound.*

Seeming satisfied with her answer, he nodded briefly. She took in a deep breath and ordered her body to behave itself. Within minutes the carriage rolled to a stop in front of her family's residence. A townhouse that now belonged to an unknown, obscure relative who would be taking possession sometime later this year. Perhaps it had been her duty to marry quickly so as to provide security for her mother. But for Mother to set up the shenanigans tonight was beyond the pale.

Arabella took Clarendon's hand after he alighted and turned to assist her. He appeared distracted, removed from the conversation they'd just had. As Tavers opened the front door, Clarendon spoke to the butler. "If Lady Melrose is receiving, I would request an audience with her." He held out his card.

The well-trained butler never reacted to having her arrive with Lord Clarendon, nor his request to speak to her mother at this hour of the night. He merely accepted the card, bowed, and said, "I will have her ladyship's maid inquire. If you will follow me, I will conduct you to the drawing room and send for refreshments."

Clarendon waved his hand. "No need for refreshments. If her ladyship receives me, the encounter will not take long." He glanced down at Arabella. "I will call upon you tomorrow. Plan to be ready for a ride in Hyde Park at five o'clock."

She stiffened. "I beg your pardon, my lord. Perhaps I have other plans for tomorrow at five o'clock."

Nash shrugged. "Cancel them."

Oh, the man was insufferable. "Mayhap I do not wish to cancel them, *my lord*."

He studied her for a minute, his arrogant eyebrow raised. Apparently, he'd never considered that she would not fall at his feet with glee at having a strong man order her about.

"I do not wish to make an issue of a simple request."

She offered him a smile sweet enough to cause a toothache. "Ah, my lord, but 'twas *not* a simple request. It sounded more like a demand."

They glared at each other.

Realizing that Tavers stood patiently while they had this exchange, and somewhat embarrassed at having the servant witness her impertinence, she tightened her jaw then offered a slight curtsy and headed up to her bedchamber, mumbling all the way.

If this was how he intended for them to go on, then he would be in for a surprise. She was no young, silly Lady Grace, who would gaze up at him adoringly, waiting longingly for commands and guidance through her life. Even though it was her mother who had inadvertently placed them both in a position that resulted in this fake betrothal, Arabella had no intention of assuming the demeanor of a swooning debutante, eyelashes batting. Until she could rid herself of the burden that was Lord Clarendon, she would make it clear he was not her lord and master.

She rang for Sophia and paced, wondering if Mother had granted Clarendon an audience and what had been said. Being the gentleman she'd found him to be, she doubted if he would insult Mother in any way. Hopefully, Mother would use her common sense and explain that jumping in with both feet to *save* her had been unnecessary.

Before Sophia had even arrived, Arabella heard the sound of a carriage door closing and wheels rolling on the cobblestones in front of the townhouse. Either his lordship had been correct, and what he needed to say was truly not very long, or Mother had refused to see him. In any event, the maneuverings Mother had set in play tonight had thrust Arabella into an untenable situation that needed correction, and fast.

The next morning, while Sophia fixed her hair, Arabella touched the puffy dark circles under her eyes with her fingertips. Based on what she saw in the mirror, a lie-down later would be necessary if she were to present herself to Clarendon for their carriage ride looking less like a hag than she did right now.

A slight knock at her door drew her from her thoughts. Mother entered, the first time she'd seen her since the debacle the prior evening. "Good morning, Arabella. I hope you slept well."

Arabella didn't know whether to laugh or cry. *Slept well? Hardly.*

"As well as could be expected, I would think, under the circumstances." Arabella glanced at Sophia in the mirror. "That is fine, Sophia. You may leave now." The young maid curtsied and left the room.

Once the door closed, Mother went immediately on the defensive. "I am sorry for the mix-up last evening, but you must admit, Arabella, things have turned out rather well."

Arabella spun around in her chair, her mouth agape. "Rather well? I am now betrothed to a man I hardly know, who was planning on offering for another lady, who probably hates me and will soon be spewing vitriol about my virtue.

Which, no doubt, several people are already questioning." Arabella stood and circled the room, slapping her fist into her palm. "Do you think I will go through with this farce? How could you do that, Mother? And Lord Pembroke?"

Mother raised her chin. "The situation had grown dire, Arabella." She wrung her hands. "I received a letter yesterday from the new earl that his plans have changed and he will be back in England within the month. We have nowhere to go."

She dropped her hands to her sides and stared at Arabella. "What do you mean 'do I think you will go through with it?'"

"Just that. I have no intention of marrying Lord Clarendon. I can barely stand the man—although I did tell him he was tolerable—but I definitely do not want him for a husband."

"You have no choice. If you do not marry him, you will be ruined. No one will offer for you. We will be tossed out into the streets."

"Not so. The new earl has already said we were free to stay here and to also make use of the estate manor until I am settled." They had discussed this very matter several times, and Arabella had no reason to believe her mother had softened her position.

"I will not live on another's forbearance. Why, for all we know, he might have a wife and several children. I doubt very much if she would be happy with the arrangement."

"You are jumping to conclusions with no merit. Furthermore, it appears to me your only consideration was worry for your own well-being. Did you, however, consider me and my wishes? I certainly would have preferred to spend the rest of my life with someone whose very presence does not cause my stomach to roil, as does Lord Pembroke."

Her mother smirked. "Well, then it is a good thing Lord Clarendon had been in the library, because I doubt very much if you will find it difficult to sit across the table from him each morning. He is certainly not difficult to look at."

This angered Arabella further. "Yes. And he is obnoxious, arrogant, high-handed, and overbearing."

Mother tugged on the cuffs of her day gown, the gesture she always used to announce the subject under discussion was closed. "We have much to do before the wedding, Arabella."

The wedding.

The memory of the scent of sandalwood and the feel of firm muscles under his clothing brought a slight kernel of excitement to her stomach. Although, as most young maidens, she knew very little of the marriage bed, she could imagine that what took place there would certainly be much more pleasant with him than Lord Pembroke and his fat, sausage fingers.

But pleasant bed activities were not enough of an enticement to persuade her to marry the man.

Arabella took in a sharp breath. "I intend to explain to his lordship on our ride this afternoon that marriage between the two of us is not well founded. I am sure he can be convinced, and there will be no need for a wedding. Things will return to normal, I will avoid Society for a while, and all will be well."

Apparently ignoring Arabella's stance on the wedding, Mother said, "Before we begin preparations for your nuptials, however, I would like to know why another foul and grubby dog is now taking up space in front of the fireplace in the kitchen, getting in Cook's way."

Arabella groaned inwardly. She'd forgotten about the poor, straggly animal that had followed her home the prior afternoon—hours before her life had changed forever. After a bath and a bit of food, he'd looked much better, and had licked her face until she'd laughed with glee. With her penchant for strays, and Miss Aphrodite now residing elsewhere, the household currently had in residence four dogs, two cats, and a bird with a damaged wing.

"You do know it is highly unlikely that Lord Clarendon will allow all of these creatures into his house."

Why wouldn't Mother listen to her? Lord Clarendon would have no say because he would not be her husband. "Another reason I need to get this all straightened out with him. I cannot abandon those animals. That would be cruel."

"No, young lady, sensible is the word that fits. Furthermore, once you marry and move into his lordship's house, I will have Tavers release the animals in the park." Once again, she tugged on the gown's cuff. "Now it is time to prepare for your wedding."

If Arabella was considered stubborn, there was no doubt in her mind where she had picked up that particular trait. Mother was either deaf or pretending to be. To keep the peace, she would go along with her—for now. Once Lord Clarendon had come to his senses, life would return to normal.

A bit of fear nudged her. If life were to have any semblance of contentment for her, Clarendon simply *must* agree to cry off.

. . .

Nash sat very still as the solicitor explained Lady Arabella's dowry, and why the amount had dwindled since it had first been set up. It appeared Lord Melrose had played fast and easy with his money. After that was gone he'd dipped first into the money set aside for his wife should he pre-decease her, and had then pilfered a chunk of his daughter's dowry. Her original amount of three thousand pounds had been reduced to a little more than five hundred.

Five hundred! Rumor had it that Lady Grace's dowry had been six thousand, and he'd depended on that to infuse some life into his estate. In addition to the lack of funds he now had available to him, most likely he would need to support his mother-in-law, since her portion was gone, and when the new heir returned, she would be without a home.

"I am sorry to be the bearer of bad news, my lord. I had cautioned the late earl that things were becoming dire, but even during the year he'd been ill, he somehow managed to find ways to wager." The solicitor tugged at his neckcloth.

"Tell me, Mr. Manson, how has Lady Melrose fared the year since his lordship died? The few times I've seen Lady Arabella, she seemed well turned out, and I assume they maintained their household and staff."

The solicitor laid the pen he'd been fiddling with on the desk in front of him. "That is another reason Lady Arabella's dowry is only five hundred. Once his lordship died, and against my advice, the trust fund passed into Lady Melrose's name. Food, household supplies, staff salaries, and clothing have been paid from that fund. Lady Melrose continuously assured me that Lady Arabella would make a successful match and their money problems would be at an end."

This was certainly a dilemma. While his situation was nowhere near as unfortunate as Lady Melrose and her daughter, he still needed to put some money into repairs on the Suffolk manor house. He also had plans to improve on the land so his tenants could produce more. The returns he'd been receiving from his steward had dwindled each year, much like his betrothed's dowry, only he hadn't been frittering the money away on gaming and other pursuits.

Well, there was nothing to be done for it. He would have to make do with what he had, and as soon as the blasted wedding was over, he would return to Suffolk and see if he could figure out how to make his estate more profitable.

After they worked out the contracts, Nash headed to White's to cap off the meeting with a whiskey. Soon it would be time to pick up his betrothed for their carriage ride in Hyde Park. The two of them together would help squash any rumors that might have started about last evening. Although Lady Arabella had not been his chosen bride, nevertheless now she was, and he did not want his future countess's reputation sullied.

He settled into a chair and signaled for a drink. He'd only taken a sip when Mr. Edmund Kilroy plopped himself into the seat across from him. The man had been an annoyance to Nash since their days at Eton. Never very popular with the other fellows, Kilroy tended to link up with whatever group was badgering a lone student. He joined the harassment, vicious at some points, always looking for praise from the group bully. One semester Nash had been the chosen one to be tortured. The following year, Kilroy had attempted to befriend him. He'd had no use for the man.

"Were I you, I am not sure I would be walking these halls. At least without sufficient protection." Kilroy moved his mouth in a stupid grin. "You cost several men a great deal of money by switching brides last night."

Not wishing to discuss the situation, especially with Kilroy, who was known for gossiping as much as the ladies, Nash grunted and took another sip of his drink.

"What happened, man? It was well known that you were all but leg-shackled to Lady Grace."

Nash placed his now-empty glass on the small table alongside him. Since Kilroy had made his visit disagreeable by his presence, it was time he made his way home to prepare for his ride with Lady Arabella. He stood and glowered at the man. "Whom I choose to marry—not leg shackle—is my own, and the lady in question's, business."

"I hear you were forced to offer for her because her virtue was in question." The odious man wiggled his eyebrows which gave rise to a swift surge of anger pulsing through Nash's body.

He leaned down and placed his hand on Kilroy's shoulder, pressing firmly enough that the man winced. "Should I hear any more comments from *any* source about my betrothed's virtue or lack thereof, I will take it as a direct insult to me and personally seek you out and thrash you." He squeezed harder. "Is there anything about that statement you find unclear?"

Kilroy shook his head.

"Good." Nash straightened and strolled away, the slight altercation with Kilroy not assuaging the anger at the man's comments. He still felt like thrashing someone.

Truthfully, part of his anger rose from his financial situation. The money he'd counted on would not be there, and he would have to work hard not to direct his anger toward his bride. Not that it was her fault, of course. The earl had left his wife and daughter in an untenable position. Lady Melrose had attempted to right their circumstances by marrying her daughter off to—from all accounts—a wealthy earl. Except her bumbling had resulted in her marrying off her daughter to the wrong earl.

He had no sooner handed his hat, gloves, and cane to his butler, Quinn, than his mother hurried down the stairs, her face flushed. "There you are, Nash. I have been waiting all morning and most of the afternoon to speak with you. Whatever happened at the Ashbourne ball last eve?"

Nash pinched the bridge of his nose. How did one tell one's mother to please retire to her bedchamber to allow him time to compose his thoughts before he began a lengthy explanation of that which still confused *him*?

"If you will join me in the library, Mother, I will be happy to answer any of your questions." He followed her down the corridor. Once they entered the library, he headed straight for the sideboard and poured himself another whiskey. "Would you care for a sherry?" When she shook her head, he added, "Tea?"

"No. What I would like are some answers."

He settled into the soft leather chair behind his desk.

"I assume from your demeanor that you've heard I became betrothed last night." He took a long, slow swallow of the liquor.

"I did. However, not to the woman I assumed would be your chosen bride. Not Lady Grace, but Lady Arabella, the late Earl of Melrose's daughter! I wasn't even aware you two knew each other."

"We did." Deciding to keep to himself the fiasco in the park yesterday afternoon, he answered, "We danced a couple of times. She is also a friend of Eugenia's. I've seen her several times at Devon's townhouse."

"And based on that scant contact you decide to spend the rest of your life with her?" His mother's voice rose a couple of octaves.

He eyed her over the top of his glass. "Be careful, Mother. The decision as to whom I marry is mine alone."

She waved her hand. "Of course, it is. I am not questioning your choice—"

"Aren't you?"

Mother sighed. "All right, perhaps a bit, but I feel very confused. Although you hadn't come out and said so, I was of the impression that you would be offering for Lady Grace."

"The idea had crossed my mind." He was reluctant to admit, even to his own mother, that he'd been duped into offering for the wrong girl. Although, most likely she had already been told the story of how they'd been discovered locked in an embrace in a dark library, in the middle of a ball.

"If you have been listening to well-meaning friends, I will attempt to explain as best I can. Lady Arabella came into the Ashbourne's library during the ball, seeking her mother, from whom she had received a note. I was there to gain some quiet. When she determined her mother was not there, she turned to leave and stumbled. I caught her, and the door opened to several people taking in the scene."

Mother sniffed. "Well, that certainly sounds as though the girl set it up."

Nash stiffened. Not even from his mother would he accept criticism of his betrothed. "No, she did not. She was as shocked and dismayed at being discovered in there as I was." He stood and walked around the desk, resting his hip on the edge. "I did the only thing I could to avoid her complete ruination and offered for her. It is done. She will be my countess, and I expect everyone to accept her as such. I will take her driving this afternoon so the entire world can see that we are both happy."

"Are you?"

"What?"

"Happy?"

Was marriage a place where one looked for happiness? All he had been searching for was a woman to be his countess, run his household, and rear his children. He'd had no desire for romance, love, or the elusive "happiness," though contentment did rank high on his list.

Now, without the funds Lady Grace would have brought, contentment might be a dream he needed to chase for a while. So far, he had kept their precarious situation to himself, and Mother's lack of knowledge in that regard would remain that way. There was no reason to burden her with that information.

But to appease the woman who had birthed and raised him, he would give her the answer she hoped to hear. "Yes, Mother. I am happy."

Chapter Five

Arabella tugged on her gloves as she descended the stairs to join Lord Clarendon at the entrance hall where he chatted amiably with Mother. Despite the unseasonably cool weather and the threat of rain, he had arrived promptly at five o'clock to escort her on a ride through Hyde Park. Apparently, whatever he and her mother had discussed the night before had not put them at odds.

He turned toward her, and something flickered in his eyes that she was unable to identify. Or perhaps she imagined it. Once again, she was mindful of his appearance. His dark blue woolen tailcoat brought depth to his blue eyes. The rest of his ensemble, starched cravat, well-fitting breeches, blue and silver waistcoat, along with well-polished Hessian boots, spoke of a young, wealthy, titled gentleman calling on his betrothed.

She shivered, not at all comfortable with that designation, and anxious to have all of that resolved. "My lord," Arabella offered a curtsy.

Clarendon bowed. "Good afternoon, my lady. Are you

ready for our ride?"

Nodding stiffly, she took his arm and they left the house, Mother's gleeful farewell echoing in Arabella's ears.

A four-wheeled curricle, with two lively Cleveland Bays tossing their heads, stood in front of the townhouse. Clarendon helped her into the vehicle, then strode around the front and joined her. "Comfortable?"

"Yes, my lord."

He snapped the ribbons and the horses moved forward, the clopping rhythm of their hooves on the cobblestones matching the pounding of her heart. What would she say to this man? Except for their recent fiasco, they were strangers, yet it was expected of her to behave as an engaged woman. The sooner she disavowed him of that idea, the better she would feel.

"Since we are betrothed, my dear, perhaps I can convince you to leave off with the 'my lord' and call me by name?"

No time like the present. "Yes, Clarendon." Goodness, was that her voice? She sounded like a squealing mouse with a cat on its tail.

He grinned. "Actually, I prefer Nash."

"Nash?"

"Yes, my given name. Once I assumed my father's title, for all the world, I was Clarendon. However, my mother and sister have never relinquished the name I answered to for years."

"And now you wish me to use that name, as well?" *Dear God.*

He studied her from under thick, dark eyelashes. Was there no part of the man not attractive?

"Unless that makes you uncomfortable?"

Uncomfortable? She wanted to jump from the curricle and run screaming back to her house. To sanity. "No, my lo— Nash. I am not uncomfortable at all."

Liar.

She cleared her throat. "However, there is something I'd like to discuss that does make me uncomfortable."

One arrogant eyebrow rose.

"I must insist, as I did last evening, that there is no need for a betrothal. If you wish to pretend to be engaged for a—very short—period of time, I believe that will be sufficient to ward off any talk of 'ruination.'"

"No."

A slow burning started in her stomach. "I insist."

"No."

Her fingers tightened on her parasol handle. She had to stamp down the very strong urge to smack him over the head with it. "I think I deserve the right to have a say in this."

"No."

A parasol would not be strong enough. Perhaps a heavy rock along the pathway would suffice. Using two hands she could probably lift it.

"Smile," he said, nodding to three older ladies of the *ton* passing them by.

She gritted her teeth, moving her mouth into a semblance of a smile. A Hyde Park afternoon ride was famous among the Quality. The latest fashions were flaunted, and the most recent *on dits* shared and remarked upon. Marriage-minded mamas displayed their daughters to their best advantage while taking note of the young gentlemen, assessing wealth and titles. The idea was to see, and be seen.

Like all other young ladies of Society, Arabella had accepted her share of carriage rides. Oftentimes with her mother, once or twice with a gentleman and her maid, and many times with friends.

This ride was like no other. The minute their carriage joined the queue, heads turned in their direction and fans rose to cover gossiping mouths. Arabella refused to succumb to the desire to duck her head. Instead, she raised her chin and smiled in the direction of the carriages they passed.

"Good girl. Do not let them intimidate you." Nash spoke to her out of the side of his mouth, keeping his eyes on the carriage in front of them.

"I have no intention of allowing any such thing." The statement would perhaps be more benign had her voice not snapped with anger. Who were these people to judge her?

"I believe conversation would be pleasant." Nash turned to her and smiled. "Remember, the purpose of this ride is to assure all is well. As a newly betrothed couple, we are supposed to be enjoying ourselves. Please forgive my poor manners, but right now you look as though you could snap the handle of your parasol in half. Or at least strike someone over the head with it. Hopefully, not me."

"The thought did cross my mind, but I feel it is not strong enough to do sufficient damage to your hard head. Just because we are in full view of the gossipers of the world, do not think I have accepted your edict on marriage. We will discuss this further when we leave the park."

Arabella attempted a smile for the gawkers. Then, thinking about the ridiculousness of it all, she gave Nash a genuine grin. Again, the same look flitted across his face she'd witnessed in her entrance hall. Whatever was that all about?

"Actually, I am enjoying myself." Startled, she realized it was true. The threat of rain had diminished, and sun peeked out from behind now-scattered clouds. With the sun visible, the air had warmed up a bit. She rode alongside a handsome man, in a stylish carriage, among fashionable people. 'Twas the first time that had occurred, since all her prior male carriage companions had been men older than her mother.

Since nothing would be resolved right now, she relaxed and actually looked around. Brightly colored carriage dresses decorated the path as young ladies rode, walked, or trotted on horseback.

"Tell me a bit about yourself, Arabella." He glanced at her sideways. "I assume I am permitted to use your given name?"

"Yes, of course. Since I am friends with Eugenia, I assume you already know a little about me."

"A few things. I also know you like to take cats to the park that escape your hold and require rescue."

Arabella shifted her parasol handle from one shoulder to the other as the vehicle took a turn in the other direction. She tilted her head and smiled. "And I know you spend time at parks to be available for young ladies to ask you to rescue their animals." She tilted her head in a saucy manner and spun her parasol.

Nash grinned. "Ah, but that is not so. I was merely taking a stroll, trying to enjoy the day, when I was accosted by a screeching furry banshee, with a pretty young lady running after her in a most unladylike manner."

She flushed. He thought she was pretty? "'Tis hard for one to maintain the demeanor of a lady when one is chasing a cat in the park."

One eyebrow shot up. "I will need to take your word for that, my dear, since I have never been a lady chasing a cat in the park."

"You must excuse me if I laugh at the image of you dressed in a gown." Arabella's smile faltered. "You have an aversion to animals, then?"

"Not so. I do not dislike animals, I am merely unable to be in the presence of some without suffering a sneezing fit."

"Miss Aphrodite?"

"Indeed." He shifted to look at her. "Whatever possessed you to name that devil's spawn Miss Aphrodite?"

"You do not believe it suits her, my lord?"

He shook his head. "And you, my dear, have managed to dodge my initial question quite nicely. Tell me something about yourself."

"And then you will do the same?" Lord, she was actually flirting with him. That would not do. Flirting was the forerunner to romance, and all the entanglements following. If she were foolish enough to actually consider this arrangement—a startling thought, that—her life would no longer be her own. Before she knew it, Nash would be controlling her, which she had no intention of tolerating.

"I am the only child of the late Earl of Melrose. I'm sure you know, as most of Society does, once he died, his estate passed into the hands of a distant relative. He will be traveling here to take possession in a few months."

"So your mother told me last night. I assume that is why she was quite anxious for you to marry." Ostensibly, their shaky circumstances had been part of the conversation between Nash and Mother.

"Yes. We have been at sixes and sevens over it for some time now. I don't understand Mother's concerns. The new earl has offered to allow us to stay on once he arrives. Father left money for Mother's benefit, as well as my dowry, so her scheming to marry me off to Lord Pembroke confuses me. Although she had mentioned a few times recently that our circumstances were approaching precarious."

She drew in a deep breath and studied Nash's hands as he guided the horses around the pathway. "Another reason I feel we will never suit is I am quite fond of animals." She glanced at him sideways, but he did not react.

"What I mean is I take care of *injured* animals."

"I have heard rumors." He continued to stare straight ahead.

"Yes, well, I'm afraid what you have heard is probably true. They mean a great deal to me, and since I do not wish to discontinue my 'hobby' as my mother calls it, a marriage between us would never work."

Finally, he turned to look at her. "I am not fond of animals. Horses, yes, they have their place—which is not in my house. Cats, I am obviously allergic to, something I never knew until recently. However, as my countess, you will have enough to keep you busy without seeking out injured animals."

She fisted her hands in her lap. "My lord, your lack of hearing concerns me. May I suggest you summon your doctor to assess your deficiency? I do not intend to marry you."

His raised eyebrow had her squirming, like a child in trouble. "Indeed?" He steered the carriage around a deep hole in the ground and continued, "I will apply for a special license, which is expected in our circumstances."

Arabella's anger rose once again. "I do not wish to discuss this here, so please refrain from making sweeping statements that will only raise my ire and cause unpleasantness."

Nash's lips tightened. "I believe we have already settled the matter. If you cry off, your reputation will not recover. All my life, I have ensured that I always behave as a gentleman. I would not be able to continue in that vein if I allowed your reputation to be destroyed when I had the ability to save it." He turned in her direction. "I agree we have had our differences, but is marriage to me so contemptible that you prefer a spinster's life under a cloud of scandal?"

A spinster's life under a cloud of scandal.

A horrid situation, to be sure. Whatever funds Father had left for her and Mother's care might be enough to buy a small house somewhere in the country and sustain them for a few years. She could always take a post as a companion or governess. Not a wonderful life, to be sure, and certainly not one she would have embraced, given the choice.

Then again, if her reputation were ruined, even a companion or governess position might not be available to her. And, she would be without her animals, for sure. She shuddered to think she might be forced to approach one of the older gentlemen she'd already rejected to announce she had reconsidered his offer. Who was to say they would agree after this? And truthfully, why would she prefer to be stuck with one of them instead of the man sitting beside her?

She studied him while he waited for her answer. She could accept what fate had placed in her pathway and marry the Earl of Clarendon. Her mother would be taken care of, Arabella would be accepted in Society as his respected countess, and all these worries would vanish.

Along with her freedom.

Given his comments on her animals, worries about her and Mother's future would be replaced by others, no doubt. Additionally, there was the problem of her much-valued independence, combined with Nash's overbearing, arrogant manner. "No. Marriage to you is not contemptible," she answered. "I just do not believe we are compatible. I appreciate your offer—sincerely, I do—but I cannot see us married to each other."

He patted her hand. "Do not concern yourself. I have reconciled myself to our predicament, as you must, as well. There is no reason we cannot have a pleasant marriage."

Botheration. Just what she'd always wanted to be—someone's reconciliation.

• • •

Nash dwelt on their conversation as they moved forward through the park, nodding at passing acquaintances and ignoring the smirks and sly looks from some. Based on Arabella's comments, she was blessedly unaware of how dire the circumstances were in which the late earl had left his family. Between Nash's conversation the prior evening with Lady Melrose when she had provided the solicitor's name, and his own conversation with the man this morning,

Arabella crying off would not only ruin her reputation, but her entire life.

As unfair as the matter was, a gently reared lady ruined, with no resources of her own, was generally only able to follow one path in life—a nobleman's mistress. Lady Arabella had the body and face to survive quite nicely in that life. He tightened his grip on the ribbons at the thought of Arabella forced to earn a living at the mercy of some of the gentlemen he knew. Even if she were fortunate enough to secure employment as a companion or governess, she would be fair game to most men of the nobility. More than one gently reared woman had fallen into a disreputable life after having been taken advantage of in a lord's home.

On the other hand, young Lady Grace was well liked in Society, pretty, and came with a generous dowry. No doubt her handkerchief would be barely dry before offers for her hand started to arrive. He doubted if the chit had held a genuine fancy for him—most likely his title had been the appeal.

Arabella, on the other hand, would have been cast to the lions if he hadn't offered for her. And considering their financial situation, the lions were close to her door. Not that his funds were much better, but since he was not taken with gambling and supporting expensive mistresses, at least he had no worries about losing the roof over his head.

"If I get the special license tomorrow, I would like to move ahead with the wedding as quickly as possible."

Arabella drew in a breath and lowered her voice to barely a whisper. "If you do not wish to hear me scream and bash you over your arrogant head with my parasol, I suggest you let off with this conversation. Now."

He was as stubborn as his bride. Even if he had decided not to be the gentleman he'd always thought himself to be and marry her, he had reached the point where it had become a contest of wills.

And he never lost.

Aside from that, all that passion and fire in his betrothed would prove quite interesting in the bedchamber. No shy miss was Lady Arabella. He would have a grand time taming her and teaching her. He shifted in his seat at the thought.

They had almost made a complete circle around the park when the one person he did not wish to see appeared in front of them, going in the opposite direction in a well-sprung carriage, along with her mother.

"Lady Spencer, Lady Grace." Nash bowed to the two ladies. He couldn't help but think Lady Spencer had dragged her daughter out to be seen in Hyde Park to assure the Quality that she had not a care in the world, even if the man all of the *ton* assumed would be offering for her was now betrothed to another.

"My lord." If Lady Spencer's tone was any chillier, the flowers alongside the path would be frozen solid. Apparently not as well-mannered as her mother, Lady Grace turned the other direction and waved to someone who did not wave back. Mostly because the only thing facing the young girl was an elm tree.

Lady Spencer raised her chin and shot daggers at Arabella. "Lady Arabella. I must say I am quite surprised to see you here today. I thought after last evening's humiliation you would have enough good breeding to stay out of sight."

Arabella sucked in a breath, and Nash's hands fisted on the ribbons. He did not mind taking a few stabs for himself, but Arabella was to be his wife and countess, and he would not allow her to be insulted. Several people strolling along stopped and pretended to view the flowers. Carriages that should have been passing by slowed to a crawl as all of Society watched the play between the main characters in the latest *ton* drama.

Lady Spencer continued. "But then, one assumes if you

indeed had proper breeding you would not have disgraced yourself so last evening."

Arabella's whole body shook alongside him, and her face turned a bright red as she stared at her lap. Unsure how his betrothed would respond to such malice, given her threat before to smack him over the head with her parasol, he gritted his teeth and rested his hand on her clenched one. "Lady Spencer, any further slights cast on my future countess will be dealt with in an appropriate manner that I guarantee will not be pleasant." He snapped the ribbons and moved forward. "I wish you good day."

They had barely cleared the exit from the park when Arabella groaned and dropped her parasol, then covered her face with her hands. Her shoulders shook, and he was certain he heard muffled sobs. Bloody hell that woman had been vicious. Even though he hated a weeping female more than anything, the thought of Lady Spencer weeping would not affect him so. In fact, the notion brought warmth to his heart.

Instead of driving directly to the Melrose townhouse in Mayfair, he took Holyhead Road out of town. The further they proceeded on the road, the cleaner and sweeter smelling the air. They soon left prying eyes behind, to be replaced with disinterested Londoners returning to their homes for the dinner hour.

He fumbled in his pocket and handed Arabella his handkerchief. She mumbled her thanks. Once her sobs had turned to slight hiccups, he spoke. "I assume you are crying because that woman could have been my mother-in-law?"

Her head jerked up, her eyes wide. Once she saw his grin, she smiled, and then chuckled. "That would have been most unsettling, my lord."

He reached out and touched her lips with his finger. "No 'my lord.' Remember?"

Her cheeks were flushed, her eyes red, and from the

sound of her voice, her nose all stopped up. Instead of looking a fright, she looked adorable. Fragile, and somewhat broken, not at all as he'd begun to think of her. Something deep inside him stirred, and he quickly smothered it, replacing it with protectiveness and righteous anger on her behalf.

"I am sure you won't be troubled by her again." He raised his hand as she began to speak. "Based on what you've just witnessed, I am sure you now understand there will be no crying off. You've done enough crying.

"If we do not move forward with our marriage, you will not have the protection of my name. Incidents like that will happen on a regular basis, until you are driven completely away from Society. I know that is not fair, but that is the way of it."

Arabella twisted his handkerchief in her hands. "She is a horrid woman. I've heard her speak to others that way, but never have I been subjected to her tongue."

"Nor will you be ever again, I assure you. We will take a few more minutes to allow time to compose yourself, and then I will return you to your home. I will speak with your Mother, as I wish to settle the matter of the wedding date."

After about another fifteen minutes, he turned the carriage and headed back to Mayfair. In three days, he would be a married man. Not something worrisome, to be sure. He had no intention of his life changing in any way. Once she settled in, Arabella would be an acceptable wife. She had a definite stubborn streak, and was a bit more headstrong than he would have liked, but he was sure he could contain her and impress upon her that all major decisions would be his.

From what he'd seen, once the matter of her animals was settled, she would not bring discredit to him or his title, and hopefully, in a short time, she would be increasing. Based on what he'd felt when he held her in his arms, getting her with child would be a most pleasurable task. Something he was certainly looking forward to.

Once he got his finances in order, theirs could be a very satisfying life. After the display he'd seen from Lady Spencer, he was feeling a bit relieved that Lady Arabella's name would be the one alongside him in the marriage book, and not Lady Grace.

Feeling quite content with the way things were proceeding, he hummed to himself as he returned his future countess to her home to prepare for their wedding. Yes, with proper handling on his part, life with Arabella would be uneventful and peaceful.

Chapter Six

"You may *not* bring all these animals with you to my house!"

Angered at his words and tone, Arabella fisted her hands on her hips. "I am sorry, *my lord*, but I thought now that we are married it was also *my* house."

Shortly after sunrise, Arabella had awakened with a sore throat and a stabbing pain behind her eyes. After drinking a posset Sophia brought her from Cook, she'd staggered out of bed, feeling as bad as she had the morning after she'd drunk too much champagne at Lord and Lady Devon's wedding.

She'd had little enthusiasm for dressing in the gown she'd selected for her wedding. The material had scratched her skin, and all she'd wanted to do was crawl back into bed.

The wedding hadn't gone much better when the minister had instructed Nash to place the ring on her finger. Panicking, she'd withdrawn her hand. He'd pulled it back. She'd yanked it back again. The tug-of-war continued until the ring had fallen to the floor and rolled under the lectern. Harsh whispers between the two of them had been interrupted by the minister's well-placed cough.

Now it was mere hours since they'd said their vows. After much grumbling and complaining about the lack of time, Mother had put together a lovely wedding breakfast. A small group, consisting of long-time friends of Nash, Lord and Lady Dowding, who acted as witnesses, along with Mother, Lady Clarendon—now the Dowager Lady Clarendon—and Nash's aged great aunt, Lady Hyatt, had joined the newly wedded couple for the repast. Nash's sister, Eugenia, and her husband, Lord Devon, had not had time to attend, since they had recently retired to the country until Eugenia's confinement ended.

Arabella had pushed the food around her plate until she'd finally asked a footman to take it away, since she thought she might toss up her accounts if she had to stare at it any longer. The few sips of champagne she'd had only made her feel worse.

When Nash had looked at her with concern and asked after her health, she'd shrugged it off, hoping she was correct that it was merely bridal nerves.

The guests had all departed among kisses and well wishes, and now Arabella was preparing to move her things—and her animals—to her new home.

"Most certainly, it is also your home, my dear. But animals do not belong in houses. We can perhaps build some sort of structure for the dogs—that is a dog, is it not?" He pointed to the poor straggler to whom she had not yet given enough attention. The bath certainly had helped, but his coat was in sore need of a trim. All this wedding business had taken her attention away from the things that really mattered.

"Yes. Of course, he is a dog." She sniffed. "And he needs care."

"What he needs, Wife, is a pistol to end his miserable existence."

Arabella drew in a breath. What sort of monster had she

married? Killing animals? Relegating them to cold, lonely places outside of the house?

"I will not shoot my friends. And these animals," she swept her hand to encompass her current menagerie, "are my friends."

Nash rubbed the back of his neck. "What of that pathetic bird?"

Arabella studied the poor thing lying in the small box in her hand. As if she knew what Arabella's thoughts were, the bird fluttered her wing. "She is mostly recovered from her accident. I assume I can release her soon."

"Today?"

She raised her chin. "Tomorrow. Maybe."

This was not starting out well. What she hated more than anything was the gloating expression on her mother's face. A perfect "I told you so" look that Arabella had been subjected to most of her childhood.

However, this was important to settle here and now. She had no intention of discontinuing her rescue of all things broken and lost. She'd spent her childhood surrounded by animals who'd needed food, shelter, and most of all, love. Some creatures she'd been able to move into loving homes, others had remained under her care. The less civilized ones tended to eat well, sleep well, then take off for parts unknown.

"What I don't understand is why that cat hasn't eaten the bird." Nash eyed the ball of orange and white fluff licking her nether parts, totally oblivious to the humans' chatter. Hopefully, he was far enough away from the animal that he would not begin a sneezing session.

"I have managed to keep them apart. Besides, Cleopatra is a lovely cat. She wouldn't harm anyone."

"Cleopatra is a dead queen, and that cat would gulp your bird for breakfast if you turned your eyes too quickly." Nash stared at the ground while he walked in a circle, keeping his thoughts to himself. Arabella held her breath. This was one battle she did not intend to lose, but she grudgingly acknowledged the final word rested with her new husband.

Nash finally stopped before Arabella grew dizzy just watching him. "This is not a situation I am happy with. Not at all. Wild animals do not belong in houses. Furthermore, you are a countess, and countesses do not collect broken animals and treat them." He held up his hand as she began to speak. "I do not wish to have a lengthy discussion about this right now, since we need to leave. However, these are my conditions. The bird is released tomorrow. The dogs can stay in the house—the area behind the kitchen, that is—until I have a kennel built. Then they will live outside. The cat," he eyed Cleopatra with disdain, "will reside in the mews behind the house, but never, never, ever inside. I do not intend to live my life by sneezing my way through my days. Is that clear?"

"I am not pleased with these ultimatums, my lord, but I agree a lengthy discourse at present is not wise." She would definitely fight harder for her animals, but right now she felt as though a very large, and very fast, carriage had run over her poor body.

"Good. Let us move along. The time grows late." He turned to leave and then drew back, studying her, as if really seeing her for the first time all day. "Are you unwell?"

Tears filled her eyes. "I am afraid so. I awoke with a sore throat and headache, and it seems to be getting worse." No doubt the last thing a man wanted to hear on his wedding night was his wife was ill.

He moved toward her and placed his hand on her forehead. "My God, you are burning up with fever, Arabella."

She nodded, the slight movement causing her head to pound. "May we move along? I feel as though I need to lie down."

"Tavers," Nash shouted as he headed to the entrance

hall to seek the butler. "Have my carriage brought around immediately. Lady Clarendon is ill, and I need to get her home as quickly as possible."

Home. The word sounded as odd to Arabella's ears as her new tittle did, since this had always been home. Now she belonged to Lord Clarendon, and consequently, home was his townhouse. Her head too muddled to sort it all out, she took a few steps, and called out, "Nash!" She stumbled and he was right beside her, wrapping his arm around her waist.

She looked up at him. He seemed very far away. "I don't feel well at all."

"I know." He scooped her into his arms and strode down the corridor. "Is my carriage ready?"

"Yes, my lord. The driver was in the process of bringing it around when I sent word for him to hurry."

Mother followed them, wringing her hands. "Will you be all right, Arabella?"

"She will be fine." Nash swept through the door Tavers held open and descended the steps.

"My animals!" Arabella barely got the words out.

"They will remain here until you are better. Now I must get you home, into bed, and summon a doctor."

Arabella rested her very heavy head against Nash's chest. Her clothes scratched, every part of her body ached, and she still felt as though she might completely embarrass herself by bringing up what little bit of food she'd consumed at the breakfast.

Nash placed her into the carriage and followed her in. She wobbled a bit until he settled beside her then drew her onto his lap.

"This is not proper," she mumbled into his neck.

"I am your husband. You look as though you will slide to the floor any minute." He grabbed a blanket from underneath the padded seat and covered her with it. Tapping on the ceiling of the coach, he leaned back as the coach moved forward.

"I am very warm. Perhaps we can remove the blanket?"

"I don't think so, Arabella. If you have a fever, you are better off covered."

She hated being told what to do, and if she wasn't feeling so miserable she would have fought him on the matter. But never had she felt so weak. A lone tear slid from her eye and traveled down her cheek. Within minutes several others joined it until she was having a hard time controlling her sobs.

Her wedding day. She'd only had three days to plan it, she was married to a man she hardly knew, their interaction so far had not been promising, she had never felt so sick in her life, her animals were left behind, *and* she was to be placed into a bed in a house she'd never even visited.

Nash tilted her chin up. "Don't cry, sweetheart. I'll get you home, and Sophia can help you into bed. I've already sent word for the doctor to attend you. It will be all right."

When she continued to cry, mewling like a weak kitten, he pulled a handkerchief from his pocket and handed it to her. "Blow your nose."

Lord, he was even ordering her to blow her nose…like she was a child. She stubbornly just wiped it instead, and closed her eyes.

• • •

Nash held his new wife, the heat from her fever-riddled body warming him enough that he wished he could strip off all his clothes. What a disaster. From the time the ridiculously named cat, Miss Aphrodite, had slammed into his chest, his life had gone from one mishap to another. And they all centered on the new Lady Clarendon—his countess.

A fine wedding night he would have. The chilling champagne and soft candlelight he'd ordered his valet to prepare would be enjoyed only by him. He sighed and looked out the window. Not that he was such a lecher he could not control himself until his wife recovered, but a man did expect to take pleasure in the idea of bedding his new wife. Especially this one, with her soft curves and lush mouth.

The short ride from the Melrose townhouse to his own didn't give him much time to feel sorry for himself. As soon as the carriage rolled to a stop, his butler Quinn hurried down the steps, still managing to maintain his dignity. "My lord, a Dr. Bennett has arrived and said he'd been summoned. I directed him to the library. Is Lady Clarendon ill?"

"Yes. Has her maid Sophia arrived?"

"About ten minutes ago. I sent her upstairs to my lady's bedchamber."

"Thank you." Nash handed Arabella off to a footman and alighted from the carriage. He was annoyed with the feeling of possessiveness as the tall, handsome footman placed her back into his arms.

"Where am I?" Arabella's voice was raspy, and her eyes glazed over.

Nash looked down at his bride. "We are home, my dear. Sophia has arrived and awaits you in your bedchamber. As soon as she has you settled, the doctor will attend you."

"Oh." She closed her eyes, her head tucked against his chest.

He was becoming concerned at the amount of heat radiating from her body, right through her clothes and his. Sophia awaited them outside the bedchamber door, wringing her hands. "Oh my lord, is my lady so sick?"

"Yes, I am afraid she is. Please see her settled in bed and I will have the doctor attend her as soon as you are finished." He placed her gently on the counterpane. He watched for a few minutes while Sophie removed her bonnet, gloves, and pelisse. Feeling as though he intruded, Nash left the room and headed to the library to speak with the doctor.

"My wife's maid is preparing her, doctor. She will notify us when she is ready."

"What seems to be the problem with Lady Clarendon?"

Nash ran his fingers through his hair. "We married just this morning, and—"

"Felicitations, my lord." The doctor nodded.

"Thank you. It came to my attention at the wedding breakfast that my wife was not herself. When she assured me it was no more than bridal nerves, I dismissed it. Then when we were about to leave her mother's home, she said she did not feel well. When I touched her forehead, she was quite hot. She then mentioned a sore throat and headache had been troubling her for most of the day."

"*Hmm.* Well as soon as I am able, we'll take a look at her. Was she complaining of a stomach upset?"

"As a matter of fact, she did. I also noticed she ate practically nothing at the breakfast."

Nash moved to the sideboard and poured a drink. "Would you care for a drink while we wait?"

"No, thank you." The doctor wandered the room, looking at the various titles on the bookshelves as Nash stared out the window, sipping on his drink. After about ten minutes of the two men lost in their own thoughts, Sophia entered the room.

"My lord, my lady is ready for the doctor now."

"Thank you." Nash headed to the door. "This way, doctor."

Arabella looked so small in the huge bed. His stomach tightened at her paleness of face and the way she picked at the covers, seeming to be unclear as to where she was. "Arabella?" He sat alongside her and took her hand, his heart thumping at the heat that came from her flesh. "The doctor will examine you now. I will wait outside."

She tugged on his hand. "No. I'm frightened. Stay here. Please."

"Certainly." He moved off the bed, and the doctor moved forward. The man was swift and efficient in his examination. Nash stayed back from the bed, watching Arabella thrash around, calling for her mother.

He was growing more alarmed by the minute. "Sophia, please send word to Lady Melrose to come immediately."

"Yes, my lord. I will go myself." The maid hurried from the room, glancing back at Arabella.

"Thank you."

Nash walked in a circle as the doctor made noises that only increased his unease. Finally, the man stood and approached Nash. "My lord, I believe your wife suffers from the grippe. Or, influenza."

"Influenza?" Nash reared back, focusing on the one word. He'd had two friends at Eton who had died from influenza, as well as his grandmother and several cousins.

"Yes. I am afraid that is what it is. I recommend leeches to rid the body of excess blood. That might help bring down her fever, as well."

"No. No leeches."

The doctor raised his chin. "That is the only accepted method of treatment for influenza."

"Well, you won't be treating *this* patient with leeches. They used that on my grandmother, and it did not help. In fact, my father was convinced it hastened her death, since she grew so weak after the procedures."

The doctor picked up his bag. "I must tell you, my lord, there is also the chance your wife suffers from nerves, combined with a common cold. We have found young and nervous ladies tend to suffer more with colds than gentlemen do. After all, they are of a weaker nature, so that is understandable."

Grateful that Arabella was too sick to hear the doctor's comments, he took him by the elbow. "I will see you out, doctor. Besides leeches, what else do you recommend for colds?" He opened the bedchamber door and escorted him out.

"Keep the room warm. Drafts are very dangerous. You might want to have her maid fix a poultice for her chest if she begins to cough a great deal. Chamomile tea is good, if you can get her to drink it." They descended the stairs. "You might use some cold cloths to bathe her body, if the fever rises."

The front door opened and Lady Melrose rushed in. "How is Arabella?"

"This is Dr. Bennett. He has just examined her and declares she has a cold." Nash glared at the doctor, warning him not to dispute him. The last thing he needed was a hysterical Lady Melrose on his hands. "Arabella was calling for you. Her bedchamber is on the second floor, the third door on the right."

Lady Melrose swept past him and hurried up the stairs.

Nash visited the kitchen and instructed Cook to fix chamomile tea and a poultice.

"Oh my lord. The poor dear, only just married and now sick." The woman shook her head. "I will also fix some broth. When my little ones had fevers, it seemed to soothe them."

He headed back upstairs to find Lady Melrose sitting on a chair next to Arabella.

"She is so warm, my lord." The woman held her daughter's hand and pushed the hair back from her forehead.

"Cook is sending up chamomile tea that the doctor suggested, as well as some broth. I will have Sophia fetch cool water and some cloths if you want to bathe her."

"Yes, thank you." She turned back to Arabella.

Once Sophia arrived with the water and cloths, Nash excused himself, not wanting to watch Lady Melrose strip his new bride and wipe her down. He did not want to feel lust for the poor girl, but considering what he had planned for tonight, his mind continued to wander in that direction.

He ate his wedding night dinner alone in the dining room, since both Lady Melrose and his mother had requested trays. He certainly did not do justice to the wonderful meal Cook had prepared for the newlyweds. After eating, he wandered to the library for a brandy and time with the book he had started but certainly hadn't planned on reading this night.

Shortly after ten o'clock he entered Arabella's bedchamber. Lady Melrose sat slumped in the chair, her eyes closed, and her head nodding. Nash touched her gently on her shoulder. "My lady, I believe you should retire for the night."

Her head came up quickly, she looked around, and then rubbed her eyes. "No, I cannot leave Arabella. She might need something in the night."

"My wife is my responsibility now, madam. I intend to stay here to see her through the night."

Lady Melrose's brows rose. "I am not sure that is proper."

He managed to keep from rolling his eyes. "We are married. You will find one of the maids outside the door. She will direct you to the room we have prepared for you and assist you in any way you need her." He reached out and took her hand, escorting her to the door. "All will be well. You need your sleep."

Glancing back at her daughter, Lady Melrose reluctantly left the room. Nash immediately undid his cravat and removed his jacket, waistcoat, and boots. He rolled up his sleeves and drew the chair closer to the bed. Resting his arm on his knees, he watched his new wife. Arabella was in a fitful sleep, tossing and turning. He felt her forehead, and she remained very hot.

He rang for Sophia and had her bring more water and clean cloths. He also shooed her to her bed, promising to fetch her during the night if he needed anything.

Once he turned the bedcovers down, he groaned at the sight of the night rail that displayed the brown nipples of Arabella's generous breasts, as well as the dark curls at the juncture of her thighs. Calling on all his resources as a gentleman, he slid the bottom of the gown up, keeping the area from the top of her legs to her neck covered, and slowly wiped her warm flesh with the cool cloth.

The chore finally done, he placed the bowl of water and cloths on the dresser. He blew out the candles and settled into the chair, planning on a long, uncomfortable wedding night.

Chapter Seven

Arabella groaned and rolled to one side. She was so hot, and her body hurt so much. What was wrong with her? She opened her eyes and for an instant panicked at the complete darkness. As her eyes adjusted, a lone figure slumped in a chair came into view. Nash.

Her husband.

She thought she remembered her mother sitting in that chair. It must have been delirium due to the fever. Here she was lying in bed in no more than a nightgown, and he sat not two feet from her. If she wasn't so sick, it would disturb her. Instead, she shifted once more, turning her back to him, and fell into a deep slumber.

She was so cold, her body racking with chills. No matter how many clothes she put on, she was still shaking. She stood in her nightclothes at the top of a hill with the wind whipping her, freezing her skin. Snow gathered at her feet, chilling her further. Was there nowhere she could go to get warm? She cried out.

"Arabella!" A gentle shake brought her out of the

disturbing dream.

"Nash?"

In the darkness, he leaned over her. "You were thrashing about and moaning."

"I'm so c-c-c-cold."

Nash lit a candle by the bedside. He was partially undressed, his hair wild from where he must have been running his fingers through it. "Your fever must be going up again. I'll get you more blankets."

"Th-th-thank you."

Nash piled two more blankets on her, but she still shook. He watched her for a few minutes, then said, "The best thing I can do to warm you up is climb into the bed with you."

"Yes. I'm really c-c-c-old."

Her eyes grew wide as he yanked his shirt from his breeches and pulled it off over his head. Golden, muscled flesh, covered with a scattering of dark brown hair down the center of his chest, disappearing into the top of his breeches. If she weren't sick, she was sure any chill would have disappeared.

He lifted the covers and joined her. "Come here." He pulled her close to him and wrapped his arms around her. She settled her head on his shoulder and laid her arm around his middle, relishing the warmth from his body. He'd been correct, he was much warmer than all the blankets he'd covered her with.

"Is that better?" He looked down at her, the darker flecks in his blue eyes illuminated by the candlelight.

"Yes, much better. I don't understand how I can be so hot one moment and so cold right after that."

"It's how your body handles a fever. When my grandmother and cousins were so sick with influenza, I read as much as I could about fevers."

"Influenza. Is that what I have?"

He hesitated, which raised her fears a bit. "No. The

doctor said it could be, but it could also be a common cold. He mentioned nerves, and considering how the last week has gone, there is a good chance this is merely a cold brought on by nerves."

"I'm not troubled by nerves."

Grinning down at her, he said, "This has been quite a different week for you than I imagine you've been used to."

"Yes. But it has been for you, as well."

"Indeed. Hopefully, I won't catch your illness. But then, I am not a nervous young lady."

Despite the pounding in her head and pain in her throat, she rallied enough to take umbrage at his remark. "I am not a nervous young lady, either."

He cupped her cheek and smiled at her in a way that made her stomach do somersaults. Somehow, she was sure it had nothing to do with her illness, either. "I think it is best if you try to return to sleep. You need as much rest as you can to heal yourself."

"Yes, I am tired." She settled against him, then asked, "Was my mother here earlier?"

"She sat with you all evening. I sent her to bed and took over your care. Now go to sleep, wife."

"Perhaps I will." Sick or no, she was reluctant to use the moniker *husband*.

• • •

Nash would probably sleep but naught this night. He'd been uncomfortable in the chair, true, but now that he lay next to his warm, soft wife, discomfort had turned into torture. At least her shaking had ceased. She had seemed coherent just now when they spoke. He remembered his grandmother delirious for most of the time she suffered from influenza, which encouraged him to think perhaps Arabella suffered from no more than a cold.

He ran his fingers up and down her arm. Glancing down at her, he caught a slight smile on her face. She was truly a lovely woman. It annoyed him that her mother had been so unsure of her daughter's appeal she had foisted old men on her. Arabella could have easily attracted a young, handsome, wealthy, and titled gentleman. Well, it turned out she had—except for the wealthy part. Certainly not to her mother's credit, but her bumbling ineptitude, instead.

Here he was on his wedding night, holding his beautiful bride in his arms, and unable to do anything to assuage the lust. He sighed and closed his eyes, trying desperately to sleep so the time would pass. Arabella turned the other direction and shoved her plump bottom into his side. He groaned.

Sometime later he woke up covered in sweat. He'd never been so hot in his life. Lying next to Arabella was like lying next to a fireplace. When he tried to ease away from her, she moved back again. Finally, unable to take it anymore, he hopped off the bed and hesitated at first, then slid his breeches down. The cool air on his naked skin felt wonderful.

Arabella began moving her arm over where he'd lain, whimpering. Well, there wasn't much he could do. He climbed back in, wrapped his arm around her middle, and drew her close to him until they were huddled together. Her nightgown had ridden up to her hips, and his very delighted erection was trying desperately to find its way inside her moist warmth. With a groan, he moved his hips back slightly, which she seemed to allow, as long as his arm encircled her.

With a sigh, and counting the horses in his stable one by one, name by name, he attempted to go back to sleep.

Nash kissed the soft skin under his lips. He pushed aside the long braid covering said soft skin and continued to kiss, lick, and suckle. The scent of lemon and lavender drifted to his nose. Only half awake, he pushed his hips against more soft, warm flesh. It had been some time since he'd awakened like this, and his raging erection told him it was time to correct that situation.

Slowly his hand wandered up the front of a sweet-smelling woman, cupping a full breast with a stiffened nipple. He encircled the nipple with his thumb and received a slight moan for his efforts. His hand slid to the other breast, and the woman shifted her lovely, plush bottom against him. He slowly opened his eyes, and jerked back. Dear God, he was fondling a sick woman!

Arabella must have awakened at the same time. She squeaked and moved so far, so fast away from him, that she tumbled to the floor. "Ouch!"

"Arabella! Are you all right?" He leaned over the side of the bed. She lay on the floor in a heap. Her nightgown was twisted around her waist, displaying beautiful, well-shaped calves and thighs. Thighs that joined right where black curly hair nestled against her alabaster skin.

"Close your eyes!" Arabella struggled to get her gown down. Nash tried, honestly he did, but he could not take his eyes off her lovely body displayed right there in front of his very happy eyes. "Nash!"

Grinning, he reached over and she took his hand. Once she stood, the gown fell in waves around her legs, covering that wonderful sight. He sighed, and she blushed a deep red. Holding her nose in the air, she climbed into the bed next to him. When she lifted the sheet, she sucked in a deep breath. "You're naked!"

"And you must be feeling better since you are aware of all these things." He reached over and rested his palm on her forehead. "You are much cooler. In fact, I would say your fever is gone."

"I do feel better. My throat is still sore and my head aches, but the aches in my body seem to have stopped. And—I'm hungry."

"Excellent. I will ring for Sophia and have her bring a tray for both of us." He swung his legs over the side of the bed and stood. Looking over his shoulder, he grinned as Arabella studied his nakedness with curiosity, despite the flush of embarrassment on her face. No shy swooning maid, his wife. All the more reason for her illness to hurry up and pass.

He pulled on his breeches and strode to the door and rang the bell for Sophia.

"Do you suppose whatever plagued me all day yesterday is truly gone already?"

Nash came back to sit on the bed next to her. "It might or might not be."

"Well, that's a definite answer."

"Sometimes you can feel better, only to have the symptoms come back again. That is why doctors say the patient should remain in bed for at least two or three days after the fever breaks."

"I will find it most difficult to stay in bed that long."

Visions of both of them naked in bed for three days had him hardening again. He would certainly have no problem keeping her entertained. He pushed those thoughts aside as a scratch at the bedchamber door drew their attention. "Come," Nash said.

Sophia entered, a slight blush on her face when she saw Nash sitting on the bed with Arabella, only wearing his breeches. "Good morning, my lady. You are looking a bit better than the last time I saw you."

"Thank you, Sophia. I am feeling somewhat better, and I would like some breakfast."

Nash turned to the maid. "Nothing too heavy. Some

porridge, and maybe a bit of toast. And tea."

• • •

Arabella chafed at his overbearing manner. "I am capable of choosing my own breakfast, my lord."

Ignoring her, he turned to Sophia. "You may leave now. As for me, please have Cook fix my usual breakfast. We will both be breaking our fast in here."

Well. This marriage was not starting off the way she had planned. He had already demanded she stay in bed for three days and ordered her breakfast for her, as if she were a child. Deciding she would have her say, she tapped him on the shoulder. "My lord, please understand I have no intention of allowing you to order my sleeping habits or my meals. I am a woman grown, and I intend to conduct myself in such a manner."

To her absolute horror, he laughed. Laughed! How dare he? She drew herself up. "I do not see what is funny about this."

Now he doubled over and continued to laugh until she had an urge to smack him over the head with the pillow. Or something hard.

"Do not laugh at me. You were the one who insisted on this marriage, and I will not be a biddable wife who listens to your every command."

"Oh my dear. That never crossed my mind. However, I told you I have done quite a bit of reading on influenza. Perhaps just this once, you can adhere to my superior knowledge?"

Arabella snorted. "Superior knowledge, indeed." She crossed her arms under her breasts.

Nash's jaw dropped, and he licked his lips.

"What?" Seeing where he gawked, she looked down and was appalled that her crossed arms were shoving her breasts upward, making the brown nipples that pressed against the fabric visible through her nightgown. She dropped her arms and pulled the sheet up to her neck.

Heat climbed from her stomach to her face. Alarmed, she realized the heat was not only embarrassment, but a sense of unease and excitement in her stomach at the look on her husband's face. "You may leave now."

He cleared his throat. "Yes. I think I will check on breakfast." He jumped up from the bed and practically ran out the door, forgetting no doubt he was without boots and a shirt. He returned within seconds and sheepishly grabbed his boots and shirt and left again.

Arabella flopped down on the bed. She did feel a lot better, but truth be known, she was still sick and weak. A few days in bed would not be a bad idea. She could have her furry friends visit, and do some needlework and read. After the stress of the betrothal and quick wedding, a little bit of rest would be a good thing.

• • •

After five days with no return of the fever, Arabella left her bed and ordered a bath. During his daily visits, Nash had told her that once she was recovered, they would take a trip to Suffolk. He wanted to speak in person with his steward and go over his books. He'd begun to believe there was something untoward going on, that had begun sometime before his father had died.

He'd sat on the edge of her bed, all arrogance and self-importance. "Once I've decided you are well enough, we will make the trip to Suffolk"

She felt the heat rise to her face at his condescension. "Once *you* have decided?" Why did he continue to behave as though she were a muddle-headed half-wit?

He looked at her, genuinely confused. "What have I done wrong this time?"

"You don't even know, do you?" Arabella had never felt the need to inflict violence upon a person. Until she'd met Nash.

"I am an adult. I can certainly determine if I am in robust enough health to travel to Suffolk."

Nash snorted. "I do not attribute wise decisions to you, Wife." He stood and straightened his jacket. "However, I believe you are most likely ready to travel." With those commanding words, he bowed and left the room. Arabella picked up the book she'd been reading and hurled it at the door.

She slapped her hands on the bed. Oh, to smack that smile off his arrogant face. She collapsed back onto the pillows. Since she was not quite ready to face Society, anyway, she was more than happy to comply with his request. She just resented the way he'd phrased his words. If only the man had *asked* if she were up to the trip, instead of telling her he would decide when they would go, and that she should be packed and ready when *he* felt the time was right.

Nash had taken to sleeping in her bed each night. He said it was because he wanted to be sure her fever didn't return. Each morning she awoke with his arms wrapped around her, his hands wandering over her body. She'd pushed his hands away, but each time it grew harder and harder to do so. Truth be known, that glance of his naked backside had started her wondering what the rest of him looked like. The feel of his warm flesh under her hands had her anticipating their joining.

She'd spent enough time around animals to know how things worked. The feelings he'd elicited from her body when he touched and fondled her had her more than ready to discover the rest of it.

It was a long day of taking a tour of the house with the

housekeeper, Mrs. McGregor, and consulting with Cook on menus for when they returned. After all of that, Arabella looked forward to reaching her bed, still feeling weak. Nash had not yet told her when they would be leaving, but since she was up and about, most likely it would be soon. When she questioned him, Nash assured her that any remaining weakness would be the last symptom to disappear. He also took that opportunity to remind her she had grumbled about spending three days in bed.

Now she sat in front of the mirror in her new bedchamber, studying her expression. She was certain this would be the night. Sophia had just left her after helping with her bath and brushing her hair into a shiny gloss that fell in waves to caress her shoulders. She wore a lovely new night rail—white, with small pink flowers embroidered along the scandalously low neckline. Her husband would be pleased with her appearance.

Attempting to distract herself, she looked around the room. During the time of her illness, she hadn't paid much attention to her surroundings, keeping the bed drapes closed most of the time while she'd taken one nap after another.

Her things had been moved into the dowager countess's former space. During one of their conversations when he'd visited her, Nash had told her she was free to redecorate and rearrange to her own taste. She did not see that much needed to be done. The walls had been covered in tasteful green and rose silk wallpaper. The highly polished wooden floor was partially covered by rose and green patterned carpets.

All the wood trim in the bedchamber, along with the fireplace, had been painted white. The space had been brought together with draperies and bedding in white, rose, and green. With her own belongings now in the wardrobe, perfumes and creams lined up on the dressing table, and her favorite pens and journal adorning the small escritoire tucked into a corner, she felt very much at home.

The sounds of Nash moving around the room and speaking with his valet next door reminded her of the fact that after tonight she would be his wife in truth. Mother had assumed this would be the night Nash would insist on his husbandly rights, since she'd been up and about all day, and she'd come to offer a bit of motherly advice. The short, hurried words she'd practically whispered had made it difficult not to roll her eyes. "Just do your duty. Lie still, don't complain, and it will soon be over."

Her eyes flew to the door between their rooms as it slowly opened.

Chapter Eight

Nash tightened the belt on his banyan and ran his fingers through his hair. He'd given his bride enough time. If he waited much longer, he would most likely have absolutely no control when he finally bedded her, since the last few mornings he'd had a very hard time keeping his hands off her.

He opened the door connecting their rooms to find her sitting in front of the mirror. He licked his suddenly dry lips. Her golden-brown hair cascaded over her shoulders to rest halfway down her back in waves. A slight flush rose to her cheeks as she regarded him with her hazel eyes.

Either she was cold or his appearance had already stirred her, since her nipples were prominent against the silky material of her nightgown. Seeing where his eyes had wandered, she wrapped her arms around her breasts, covering the lovely sight.

"No. Don't do that." He walked toward her and extended his hand. Looking up at him with a combination of curiosity and determination, she placed her small, delicate hand in his. He drew her to her feet and moved her forward until she was almost flush against him.

"You are a beautiful woman, Arabella." He ran his fingers through her hair, dragging the locks over her shoulder to rest on her breasts. His palm slid down her arm to her hand, where he entwined their fingers together. Slowly, he bent his head and took her lips in a soft, gentle kiss.

Their first kiss of substance.

She was all honey, lemon, and woman. The scent from her bath and hair drifted over him as he cupped the back of her head and nudged her lips with his tongue. After some hesitation, probably not sure what he wanted, she slowly opened her lips, and he delved in. Now he tasted mint that mingled with her other scents, offering a bouquet of fragrances uniquely Arabella.

He pulled away from her and held her shoulders. "Are you feeling well?"

"Yes."

"Frightened?"

"No. Should I be?"

"If you trust me not to hurt you, now or ever, it will go much smoother. I want to make this as pleasurable for you as it will be for me." He scooped her up and carried her to the bed. Laying her down gently, he joined her, resting his head on his left hand as he studied her.

"Do you realize your eyes almost match your hair in color?"

Arabella nodded. "I've been told that. I fail to see it myself, however." She startled and inhaled deeply when his finger began to trace the soft skin on her cheek.

"Relax, Wife. We've spent many a night in this bed together."

"I am not nervous." She glanced sideways at him. "Perhaps curious."

For days now he'd ached—literally—to introduce her to

the pleasures that awaited them. And truth be told, he was becoming a little frantic himself to take her as a husband takes his wife.

He smiled slowly and bent to capture her lips in another gentle kiss. This time she willingly opened her mouth before he asked. She was a fast learner, his wife. No surprise there. He placed his arm around her waist and pulled her the slight distance between them until her body rested flush against his. He held in a moan at the feeling of her soft breasts pressed against his chest. The warmth and lushness of her body set his heart to thumping.

Her breathing seemed to increase, and she slowly moved her hand up his chest.

"Yes. Touch me." He nibbled on her earlobe then sucked lightly.

Of course, he'd had his share of courtesans and opera dancers, but making love to the unschooled woman to whom he'd pledged his life was a heady experience. Her innocent touch, her soft breaths, her sweet lips on his chest, all reminded him of the precious gift she gave of her body.

With deft fingers born of undressing many females in his time, he kept her lips busy while he slowly moved his hand up, underneath her gown, until it rested at her waist. He caressed her plump bottom, bringing a slight, but definite, sigh from her lips. "Let's take this off. You'll be more comfortable," he murmured in her ear.

She shifted and allowed him to pull the garment over her head. He tossed the gown away while she covered her breasts again. He took both of her hands in his and removed them, placing them on his shoulders, then bent to take one pouting nipple into his mouth. He swirled his tongue over the bead, taking light nips that he soothed with his lips.

Her hands moved to tangle her fingers in his hair, pulling him closer. "That feels good."

"Sweetheart," he murmured against her breast, "it only gets better from here."

. . .

Arabella shivered, but not from the cold. Even though her nightgown had been deftly removed by her husband, the warmth of what he was doing with his wicked mouth was slowly raising her temperature. She rubbed her foot alongside his leg, and the coarse hair felt strange against her skin.

With a final lick, Nash released her breast and moved to the other one. Slowly, his hand made its way down her body until it rested on her hip, kneading it gently. Everywhere he touched brought shivers and gooseflesh to her skin. The ministrations to her breasts caused strange, tingling feelings to the area between her legs. Where his hand now rested.

When had he moved it?

She tried not to think about this man, who only a little more than a week ago she'd barely known, touching her so intimately. But oh, how wonderful was his touch!

Thinking he would enjoy her caresses as much as she was enjoying his, she returned her hand to his chest since he seemed to like that when she did it before. The soft hair was in contrast to his sinewy muscles. She skimmed her fingernail over his flat nipple, and he jumped, but smiled as he said against her mouth, "Don't stop."

With his fingers, he nudged her thighs, which she took to mean he wanted her to open her legs. "That's it, honey." He sucked in a breath. "You're already wet for me."

Not sure if that was good or bad, she attempted to close her legs and whispered, "I'm sorry."

He grinned. "No, sweeting. That's good. It means your body is preparing yourself for me."

"Oh. Should I be doing something to prepare you?"

Instead of an answer, he groaned, took her hand, and moved it to his man parts. Goodness it felt strange. Soft and hard. Silky and smooth. She held it like she would her parasol, her hand wrapped around it. Nash placed his hand over hers and moved it up and down. "Yes." He gritted his teeth. "Just like that."

This was all very strange. The feelings, the sensations, touching her husband in a very odd place while he did the same, excited her, made her long for something else that she knew would be even more pleasurable. Her suddenly restless legs kept moving, and the need to press the area between her legs against something hard overwhelmed her senses.

Surrounded by Nash's heat and his scent, everything else receded as she concentrated on him and what he was doing to her. The feel of his barely covered body resting on hers was comforting and exciting at the same time. The silk of his banyan contrasted with his skin. Skin that was not as soft as hers, but coarse, lightly covered with hair.

Her restlessness increased, and all her focus centered on the place between her legs. Heat rose from the spot to travel up her body, washing over her like a warm bath. Nash seemed to understand what she wanted, because he began circling, pushing with his thumb, right where she wanted it the most. "Do you like that, sweeting?"

"Oh yes." The words came out as a sigh. She opened her eyes to see him staring at her, his lips quirked in a slight smile. His eyes had darkened, and his breathing had increased as much as hers.

He moved his hand so a finger slipped into her opening. He nibbled on her lips, whispered words of encouragement, how much he desired her, how beautiful she was, how he wanted to make her his.

At the same time, he continued his attentions to her breasts, suckling, licking, nipping, then soothing. That, combined with what he was doing with his fingers had her heart pounding and her breaths coming in short pants, as if she were running a race. What was happening to her body? She pressed against his fingers, a slight moan escaping from her dry lips. She reached, searched, eager for something she knew she wanted. Nay, desperately needed.

She ran her fingers through his hair, tugging, needing something to hold onto while all her senses were heightened.

"Relax, sweetheart. Just let go." He murmured in her ear, his own breathing erratic. He moved farther over her body, his leg between hers as he continued to rub, stroke, and caress. "Does that feel good?"

"Oh yes. Yes. Just like that." She lost all sense of time and place. And modesty. She opened her legs wider, then shut them to press against his hand.

"Enough." With a strangled cry, Nash removed her hand from his member. "If you keep that up, I will disgrace myself."

His words flitted in and out of her mind, while she concentrated on what was happening to her body. She cupped his face in her hand and pulled him in for a searing kiss, this time using her tongue to nudge his lips apart.

His smiling lips.

She had no idea what was happening, what he was doing, where he was bringing her, all she knew was that her body was spiraling out of control. She sensed she was headed toward something wonderful. Nash's finger pushed into her opening, sending her higher, her heart hammering in her ears. A fine sheen of sweat covered her body, which would have embarrassed her had she presence of mind. Instead, all of her concentration was focused on a spot to which she'd never given more than a passing thought.

She licked Nash's flat nipple, sending shivers through his body. Salt. Lemons.

Pleased with herself, she licked it again. Then, a tiny

flicker started where his fingers worked, and then grew, until she felt as though she were on a ship that was about to ride a gigantic wave. She strained to reach the top, to crest what was out of reach, pushing against his hand. "Yes, harder please."

She barely got the words out when she came crashing down, flooding the shore. She moaned as wave after wave of intense pleasure washed over her, gooseflesh covering her body, until she curled her legs up and turned onto her side, facing Nash who continued to stroke her until her body stilled and she felt as though her bones had melted.

After a few moments, she sighed. "Oh my."

Nash stood and shrugged out of his banyan. Although she struggled to bring in air, she still noted the perfection that was Nash's body. She'd seen statues in books and in the museum, but nothing compared to this flesh-and-blood man. His muscles rippled as he moved toward her.

Through lowered eyelids, she took in the part of him with which he intended to enter her body. Had she any energy left, she would have scooted from the bed. He was so large! Instead, she merely whimpered as he climbed back onto the bed. His knee nudged her legs apart, and he settled himself there.

He kissed her deeply, his strong hands holding her head, anchoring her to the bed. His body full on top of hers brought back some of her earlier feelings. Smoothing back the damp curls from her forehead, he kissed her again, this time more gently. He pulled back and stared into her eyes, then moved his mouth to her ear. "Relax. I will try my best not to hurt you, although you might feel a twinge of pain."

Pain? She remembered Mother mentioning something about pain, but at the time Arabella had thought she'd meant the pain of embarrassment.

That part of him she'd held so snugly nudged at her center. He eased in, but kept her distracted by kissing her jaw, her chin, the soft sensitive skin under her ear. Whispered words tumbled out of him as he moved in farther until he stopped and looked down at her.

"This will only hurt for a minute."

Before she could ask him anything, he surged forward, and a sharp pain brought a squeal from her lips and tears to her eyes. Nash placed his forehead on hers, his soft, sweet breath coming in gasps. "Are you well?"

As fast as the pain had come, it left just as quickly. "Yes. I think I am."

"Good." He bent to kiss her as his hips moved so his shaft slid in and out of her. At first it felt odd, then quite pleasurable. Her fingernails dug into his shoulders as the tension from before began to build again.

"I'm sorry, honey, I've waited too long, and I'm afraid this will be over rather quickly." No sooner had the words left his mouth than he stiffened, and with a groan, lowered his head to her neck and pulled her tightly against him, moaning her name softly. After a few moments, he said, "God, I wanted you so bad. I apologize."

"For what?" She ran her fingers through his hair, the sandalwood smell strong on her fingers.

Nash rolled off her and pulled her against his side. "In time, you will understand."

"Is it always like this?" She continued to play with his hair. "I mean, will I have those feelings every time we do this?"

He smiled. "You mean when we make love?"

His eyes sparkled, bringing the now-familiar fluttering to her lower parts. Lord, how could he look so pleased, so satisfied with her question? Or perhaps he was pleased and satisfied with their joining. She certainly was.

He took her hand and kissed her knuckles. "Yes, my love. If we don't allow angst into our bedchamber, it will always be like this."

My love? That certainly frightened her.

They lay for a while in each other's arms as their breathing returned to normal and a chill covered their bodies. Arabella shivered. "Should we not put our clothes back on?"

"'Twill actually be warmer without clothes, as long as we huddle together with the blankets over us." He reached down and drew up the bedding. "You are just recovering from an illness, so the extra warmth is a good thing."

Nash ran his fingertips up and down her arm, bringing a sense of peace she hadn't felt since before the debacle in Ashbourne's library. This part of marriage was certainly much more interesting and enjoyable than the rest of it had been thus far, since his arrogance did not extend to their bed activities. She turned her head slightly to see Nash staring at her. A bit disconcerted at his attention, she said, "I am concerned about my animals and how they have been faring at Mother's house while I've been sick."

It troubled her that her illness had taken her away from her furry friends. She'd asked after them a couple of times, but now she had a desire to actually see them.

Nash closed his eyes and shook his head. "Your mother has asked every day when they could be brought from your former home. I believe they will be arriving early tomorrow. I did not want them here while you were sick." He touched her shoulder and eased her onto her back so she looked directly at him. "Remember they will be housed outside."

She bristled. The arrogance was back. However, a switch in subjects was required so as not to ruin the relaxed mood. "Should we not discuss our trip to Suffolk?"

"What is it you wish to know?" He continued to stroke her arm, then placed a soft kiss on her head. Was this normal behavior after intimacy? It felt rather nice, actually. Somehow, she had assumed once it was all over, he would merely roll over and go to sleep. She could learn to enjoy this part of it as much as the other.

"When are we leaving would be a good place to start."

"Perhaps the day after next. I want to be sure you are fully recovered before we travel. That will give you a day to have Sophia prepare."

"I am fully recovered."

One arrogant eyebrow. "Will this be another argument?"

She smiled. "Not unless you make it so."

Choosing to ignore her words, he said, "The trip there will only take one day, unless you are fatigued, then we can stop overnight halfway there. I would like to spend at least three or four days meeting with my steward, staff, and tenants. Perhaps plan for a week. We have social commitments we need to see to here in London." He leaned back and looked at her when she groaned.

"What?"

"I am not looking forward to a return to Society. I am sure there will be much in the way of remarks, glances, and other unwelcoming things for us to deal with."

"There will be no problem. We are married now. I am quite sure our situation will be no more interesting than any other so-called scandal."

"I hope you are right." The words barely got out around her yawn.

"Now I wish for you to sleep, Wife. You still need more rest than normal."

A low growl in her throat was her only response to his command. Her thoughts drifted away from trips to Suffolk and appearances at balls and other social events. What they'd just shared had been nothing like she'd ever imagined. Quite exciting. Perhaps they could do it again tomorrow, or would her pompous husband think her a wanton if she suggested such a thing?

She yawned once more, her eyes tearing up. It had been

such an eventful couple of weeks. Their betrothal, quick wedding, her illness, and now their joining as true husband and wife. Also, it seemed odd to be lying fully naked next to her new husband in bed. The last thought she had as she drifted off into a restful slumber was she felt quite comfortable. She was not restricted by clothing, her husband's large body kept her warm, and she began to hope that perhaps this marriage might be as tolerable as the last hour had been pleasurable.

Chapter Nine

"What the bloody hell!" Nash bolted up from his prone position as hairy bodies jumped on the bed, barking, growling, and using their teeth to grab the blankets off him and Arabella. "Arabella!" He began shoving the dogs from the bed to the floor, but they bounded up again.

His wife sat up, laughing and rubbing the animals. "Good morning, my friends."

He looked at her aghast. Yes, she was indeed laughing. Stark naked, looking well-loved, and laughing! Her hair was in disarray, she bore a slight beard burn on her shoulder's lovely skin, and all he wanted to do was climb on top of her and repeat last night's pleasure. Instead, he was tossing bodies off his bed.

"Arabella, get rid of these animals! I told you they were not to be in the bed." He looked toward the open door. "Who the devil let these demons in?"

Sophia's shaky voice came from the corridor. "I am sorry, my lord, they followed me up the stairs and raced in as soon as I opened the door."

Between laughs, Arabella said, "It is all right, Sophia. They're excited to see me." She glanced at Nash. "They usually sleep in my bed."

Nash hopped off the mattress, cringing as he stepped on a creature who no doubt thought himself a canine, when he was no more than a woolly rat. Reaching for his banyan, he shrugged into it, tying the belt so tight he winced. The devil take it, the bedroom was a disaster. Two of the dogs were chasing each other around the room, jumping on the bed and then off again as they continued their run.

Nash put his finger and thumb to his mouth, and holding his lips apart, let out with a loud, long whistle. Everyone stopped moving, even his wife, who stared at him wide-eyed. He opened the door to the corridor and waved. "Out. Every last one of you. Out."

Amazingly enough, the dogs all meekly lumbered past him, heads down. No, he would not feel guilty. Not even when he saw the disappointment in Arabella's eyes. "I will see a kennel built for them immediately," he fumed. "Until such time that they can be removed to the kennel, you will inform your lady's maid to be careful when she opens doors."

Arabella raised her chin. Was she unaware of the fact that she was naked, and the top part of her glorious body was in full view in the sunlight? Her hair resting against her alabaster skin had his mouth watering. She still had the flushed look from sleep, and if his morning erection grew any larger, he'd be unable to walk.

"Am I to be ordered out of the room as well, my lord?"

He rubbed the back of his neck. "No, you will not be ordered out of the room. But I told you there would be no animals in my bed." He grinned as he crossed the room and joined her. "Only me."

Flushing at his words, Arabella's voice grew deep, and her breathing rapid. "Please make it large enough so they can run and play."

"I will see to it." He looked longingly at her, then realizing she was probably sore from the previous night, reached for the gentleman within. "I will leave you to prepare for the day. I would suggest you have Sophia arrange for a warm bath for you to ease any soreness from last night's activities."

He leaned over and kissed her on the tip of her delicate nose. "I will see you at breakfast." After reaching the door, he turned back. "I plead ignorance of your normal routine. You have been having trays in your room during your illness. Do you prefer to continue that?"

"I am generally of a robust nature. I prefer a hearty breakfast and then a ride. Has my horse, Bessie, been brought from my townhouse mews?"

"Yes. I saw to it yesterday. If you have no objection, I would like to join you on your ride?"

Arabella dipped her head. "As you wish."

"Ah. But do *you* wish? Or am I in trouble with my new countess over her animals?" He gave her what he hoped was a charming smile. As much as he despised animals in the house, he didn't want to start off this marriage on the wrong foot, particularly with how things had gone the night before. He'd discovered a deep passion in his lovely wife and looked forward to unleashing that passion in the future.

"Yes. You are welcome to join me. However, I would appreciate you not telling me how I may, and may not, ride."

"Perhaps your appreciation could be shown in some interesting ways?" He lounged in the doorway, a smile leisurely settling on his lips.

She fought and failed to keep the smile from her lush lips. "I am certain I do not know what you mean."

The devil take it, she boiled his blood. "Oh, but I think you do know." He lowered his eyelids. "Have no fear, my countess, I will think of something appropriate." He winked at her, and with those parting words, left her and rang for his valet, Andrews.

Once his morning ablutions were completed, he descended to the breakfast room, surprised to see his mother sitting at the table. "Good morning, Mother. I haven't seen you at breakfast in years."

"I am traveling today."

"Indeed?" Nash filled a plate with eggs, oatmeal with sweet cream, bacon, smoked herrings, sardines with mustard sauce, and grilled trout with white butter sauce. He added two thick slices of bread to his repast and moved to his seat at the head of the table. "Where are you traveling to, may I ask?"

"I am off to visit Eugenia in Devonshire." The dowager countess took a sip from her teacup.

"Please tell me I am not chasing you from the house with my marriage." He shook out his serviette and placed it on his lap.

"No, and a little bit, yes."

"Perhaps you should explain, madam." Hungry from all the activity the night before, and battling with furry creatures earlier, Nash dug into his food as his mother spoke.

"I had planned to stay with Eugenia when her time came, but I think with all the recent changes it might be a better idea to go now."

"And why is that?"

Mother placed her serviette alongside her teacup and laid her hands in her lap. "You have had no time at all to get to know Arabella, and neither has she had time to learn about you. Your marriage was a hurried affair, and she became ill immediately. I believe giving the two of you time alone would go a long way toward helping you both."

She sighed deeply and pulled a piece of paper from her day gown pocket. "Also, just this morning a note arrived from Lady Melrose indicating she planned to take up residence here."

Nash swallowed the wrong way with this news and began to cough. Mother signaled the footman to pour a glass of water for her son. Nash took several sips and pushed his partially filled plate away from him. "Take up residence here already?"

Mother nodded. "Yes. I am led to believe she feels as though she will be asked to depart from her home momentarily, and wants to avoid any unpleasantness when the new earl arrives."

"He is not due to arrive for a month or more."

She shrugged and passed him the note. "Although she addressed the letter to me, I think you should certainly offer it to Arabella. Why Lady Melrose chose me to notify of her plans is baffling, unless she had reason to believe you and Arabella would be taking a wedding trip."

"Frankly, I don't know what to make of this. Of course, I won't have my wife's mother on the street. But one wonders what the hurry is." He opened the note and studied it. "It appears she has been notified that the new earl will be arriving much sooner than planned."

"In any event, I have decided to visit Eugenia and stay until the child arrives."

He looked up at her, frowning. "That won't be for many months."

"Yes. But her country home is much larger than this townhouse. You do not need your mother about, looking over your wife's shoulder. Arabella needs to find her own way to run the household and should not have to feel as though she needs my permission to change things. It is her house now, and she needs to feel comfortable."

"So instead you will plague Eugenia," he said with a smirk.

His mother stood and kissed the top of his head. "But of

course. I am her mother. That is my privilege."

"Much like Lady Melrose has the privilege to plague my wife." Nash pushed his chair back and stood.

She smiled brightly. "I always knew you were a bright young man."

"How soon will you leave?"

"I expect to be ready to depart in about two hours. I would like to speak with Arabella first. I don't want her to think she is chasing me away." She tapped her chin with her fingertip and studied him. "Despite how things started off, I do believe Arabella will be a good wife for you, Nash. She is older, and you won't feel the need to guide her every step."

"I agree. Though the lively visit from her menagerie this morning before I had time to even open my eyes is an issue that needs to be dealt with."

"Ah, yes. I remember growling and shouting coming from your bedchamber earlier. Cook said someone from Melrose Townhouse delivered the animals this morning." His mother tried her best to stifle her laughter but did not succeed. "I am sure you will get it all worked out. As I've already noted, you are a bright young man."

. . .

Arabella entered the kitchen on her way to the breakfast room. "Does anyone know where my dogs are?"

Cook dropped the spoon she was using to stir something over the fire. "My lady! What are you doing in the kitchen?"

"Looking for my dogs?"

"It isn't proper for you to be here, my lady. You can always send a footman with a note. However, I believe his lordship ordered Macon, one of our footmen, to take them on a morning walk."

"Thank you." She left the very flustered cook to resume

her duties and continued on to the breakfast room. It appeared her new home was much more formal than the one in which she'd been raised. Although, it did seem Nash employed more servants than her mother had. She had begun to wonder about the depletion of help at their home over the past year or so, but had never questioned it.

Nash sat at the table, his head buried in the newspaper. He glanced up and stood. "Good morning, again."

Memories of the night before flooded her, giving rise to what she was sure was a very red blush to her cheeks. How could Nash sit there like it was any other morning after the things they'd done? Then she realized, as a man, what they'd done the night before was nothing special to him, since he no doubt had bedded many other women. Her spirits drooped at that realization, hoping he hadn't found her wanting, compared to others. Shaking off her despondent mood, she moved to the table loaded to groaning with an array of breakfast foods. "Everything looks delicious."

"I had no idea what you preferred for breakfast, so I had Cook prepare several items. If there is anything else you enjoy, I will have Cook add it to the breakfast list."

"No, this is fine. Truly, wonderful." She filled her plate with eggs, toast, an orange, and bacon. Once Nash pulled out her chair for her and she sat, he waved at the footman. "Bring some hot tea for her ladyship."

Arabella leaned her head to one side. *There he goes again, deciding things for me.* "Actually, I prefer coffee in the morning."

"Really?" Nash viewed her with surprise, then turned to the footman. "Make that hot coffee for her ladyship, and I will take some more, as well."

"I guess we have a great deal to learn about each other." Arabella tapped her egg with a spoon and peeled away the cracked shell.

"I think most couples have the same task. Even if we had courted for weeks, I would still not know what you ate—or drank—for breakfast."

Of course, you could have asked.

"We received an invitation to a soiree Thursday next. We should be back from Suffolk by then. I will pass that, along with any other solicitations to you, since I assume you will be handling our social calendar?"

Arabella stopped as she raised a piece of toast to her mouth. "Oh, I hadn't thought about that. Mother always took care of those things and just told me where we were expected, and when."

"If you check with my valet, Andrews, he is apprised of events I have already accepted. Since you are now my wife, it is expected we will attend together. I am sure Andrews will not be relieved to see his control of my life at an end, but, nevertheless, you are in charge now."

It appeared at least in one area of their life there would be no interference from her husband.

Nash folded the newspaper and placed it alongside his plate. "Mother received a note this morning. She passed it along to me, and I feel you are the correct person to have it." He handed her the folded paper.

She glanced at the note. "Yes, Mother had always planned to take up residence with me when I married. I had hoped it would not be quite so soon, however."

He eyed her fumbling with the note. "It is not a problem, Arabella. We will not have your mother tossed into the street, although I doubt very much if that is the new earl's intention. However, if it makes your mother feel more secure, then so be it. She seemed to get on well while she was here during your illness.

"On another note, my mother is leaving later this morning to visit my sister and her husband in Devonshire."

"Your mother is leaving?" A small knot appeared in her stomach as she placed her hands in her lap, her appetite gone. "Is it because of me?"

"No. And she specifically mentioned that she was not leaving because of you. It is her intention to speak with you before she leaves, to assuage you of any concerns about her departure. She feels we need time to settle in together, and you need time to find your feet with regard to managing the household."

Another area where she was to be in charge. Her spirits rose. Now if she could continue on with her animals, things might actually become pleasant in this marriage. Particularly where bed activities were concerned.

"I'm sure Mrs. McGregor would be more than happy to answer any questions that arise. She has been with the family since I was in short pants. That also means she feels as though she knows what is best for all concerned. I'm afraid you will simply have to accept that." He gave her a half smile, confirming the fondness he felt for the woman.

His charming way set her to thinking. Fate had been kind to her, since he was certainly someone she was fortunate to have been caught with in a dark library. If things had turned out the way her mother had planned, she would right now be staring across the breakfast table at Lord Pembroke. She shuddered to think of every morning watching his sausage fingers stuff food into his mouth. To say nothing of having those same fingers touch her body in the way Nash had caressed her the night before.

A very familiar voice rose from outside the breakfast room door. Arabella laid her coffee cup in the saucer and stared at her mother standing in the doorway, Quinn hovering over her. "My lord, my lady, Lady Melrose has arrived."

Nash pulled out a chair for her mother. "Lady Melrose, please have a seat." He turned to the footman. "Please bring hot tea for her ladyship and see that fresh food is brought out as well."

Mother waved her hand. "No need for food, but a cup of tea would be very nice. And perhaps a small cake, or a roll of some sort."

After greeting her mother, and raising her cheek for a light kiss, Arabella continued with her breakfast, finding her appetite had once again returned to normal. Mother thanked the footman for the tea, and after fixing it, took a sip. Nash stood and bowed. "I will leave you ladies to work out the logistics."

"No, wait." Arabella jumped up and hurried after him. She caught him in the hallway as he was trying to make his escape from the house. "When will the kennel be built?"

He frowned and turned for Quinn to help him into his greatcoat. "Once I commission someone to do it." The arrogance was back.

She rested her hands on her hips. "And when will that be?"

"When I have time." He gave her a peck on her cheek and taking his hat, gloves, and cane from Quinn, left the house.

Quinn's dignified presence kept her from stamping her foot like a child.

Chapter Ten

Nash handed his belongings to the footman at the door of White's. Trying to adjust to marriage and his new life had forced him to flee the house and spend some quiet time among familiar people and things. He'd forgotten the promised ride with Arabella, but with her mother settling in, most likely she would forgo the outing.

In less than two weeks, he had married a woman he barely knew, who'd spent the time since their vows recovering from an illness. His hopes for the funds to prop up his estate had been dashed, and his mother-in-law had moved in, as his own mother moved out. He shook his head. Too many changes in too short a time period.

"Clarendon!" Lord Langley waved at him from across the room. The longtime friend was a welcome sight in view of all the adjustments with which he was presently dealing. After weaving his way across the room, nodding to various members, Nash settled into the comfortable leather chair across from Langley. The familiar walls of the club, the hum of conversation, the cup of coffee presented by a footman, and the boisterous activity surrounding the betting book all worked to soothe him, bringing familiar normalcy back into his life.

"The new bridegroom, already escaping from his bride." Langley grinned at Nash before taking a sip of coffee.

Although Nash felt a bit of resentment at his friend's remarks, there was truth in the statement. He was, indeed, escaping. Not necessarily from Arabella, but everything she represented. Change. Change on which he hadn't planned.

"I wasn't aware that you were even acquainted with the former Lady Arabella, never mind ready to offer for her. Or is there substance to the rumors floating about?"

Nash waved his hand in the air. "I pay no attention to rumors. My wife—" He choked on the word. "And I, are well. She has household matters requiring her attention this morning, and I would merely be in the way."

"As you say." Langley placed his cup in the saucer and leaned back, resting a booted foot on his knee. "On a more interesting note, it has come to my attention that a very lucrative investment is in the wind, and I have every reason to believe it is something you would be interested in, as well. From what I hear, only a select few are being invited to join in."

Langley's words brought to mind his limited funds and current financial state. His feeling of contentment slowly ebbed away. "What sort of investment, and how much?"

"Only two hundred pounds per man." Langley leaned forward and motioned to Nash to do the same. "A man will never make any sort of money from the Funds. This investment is in trade."

"Trade?" Peers did not involve themselves in trade, although Nash had known several who *had* made a significant amount of money, in a very quiet way, by investing in trade. The school of thought was, as long as a gentleman did not directly involve himself, those who mattered were happy to look the other way. "Do you have the information on hand?"

"Silks and china from the Orient. Cloth from India." Langley stopped as two members drifted by, close enough to hear their conversation. He drew out his calling card and after summoning a pen from a footman, scratched words on the back. He handed it to Nash. "There's a meeting next week. Here is the date and direction. If you are interested in hearing more, come by about eight in the evening. You can judge for yourself."

Nash took the card from Langley's hand and studied it. The location he'd written was in a part of town containing warehouses that stored goods shipped from various parts of the world. He would be remiss if he did not attend this meeting. If he used part of Arabella's dowry for an investment, the rest could be put aside to make at least some improvements for the tenants on his estate.

"Now I must leave you to your internal meanderings, as I have an appointment with my tailor. Have to keep up appearances, you know." Langley grinned at Nash and stood. "I hope to see you at the meeting. From what I've learned so far, it could be quite worthwhile."

Nash nodded. "And you believe it is possible I would be one of the chosen few?"

"I will meet you there. If you want in, it will be so." Langley winked and strode through the room.

It would certainly be smart to at least see what the presenter had to say. He stuck the card in his pocket and picked up the newspaper Langley had discarded.

Close to the dinner hour, he entered his townhouse. He had no idea where Arabella was, and everything was quiet. He headed to the library. A study of his financial records was a good idea. He would be sure to pledge the two hundred pounds at the meeting, but would only relinquish the money if he was convinced it was the best use of Arabella's dowry.

Deep in thought, he opened the library door and came to a dead stop, his nose twitching at the strong odor. "What is going on here?"

Arabella rose from a kneeling position as he shouted, the front of an apron covering her dress full of blood and mud. A cat and a small dog lay in individual baskets on the floor in front of the fire. They were both whimpering and bleeding from several gashes. If blood had not been dripping from the cat, he would have sworn it was dead. A basin of brown-stained water sat between them, and his wife held a cloth fisted in her hand. "Oh thank heavens you are home. I need your help."

"Madam, this is not a surgery, but my library. What are those animals doing bleeding all over my floor?"

Arabella wiped her hands on the cloth and moved toward him. "They are not bleeding on the floor. They are in baskets. To answer your question, Cleopatra and Hercules got into a fight with another animal who escaped. I'm afraid they both require stitches."

Hercules? This dog was the one he'd noticed earlier, that he'd thought was no more than a large rat. She'd named him Hercules? There was no doubt in his mind. His wife was daft. Perhaps he could arrange for an annulment based on lunacy.

His or hers. It mattered not. Once he told the court his story, he was sure to prevail.

"Arabella, you are not a veterinarian. You might end up killing these animals." He shook his head and placed his hands on his hips. "And you are supposed to be preparing to leave for Suffolk tomorrow."

She raised her chin and glared at him. "I have done this

sort of thing for years, my lord. I could use your assistance, but if you refuse, it will not stop me from helping them." She waved her hand. "And I am all ready to leave tomorrow."

Nash rubbed the back of his neck, still discombobulated at the scene in his neat, quiet library. "What I could use is some assurance that I will not come home to my wife performing surgery in my library. This is not the way a countess conducts herself, Arabella."

"Maybe not, my lord, but this is the way *I* conduct myself." Her eyes flashed, and she stuck out her little, stubborn chin.

He had anticipated a stronger presence in the *ton* with a wife to handle their social calendar and do all the things a countess does. His mind had conjured up pictures of Arabella involved in sewing circles to make garments for the poor, hosting dinner parties, and making and accepting afternoon calls.

Instead he was faced with a willful, hardheaded woman who refused to adapt to her new position in life. Lord what had he gotten himself into? "Perhaps that tidbit of information should have been shared with me before we said our nuptials." He stalked across the room and poured himself two fingers of whiskey.

The wet, bloodied cloth still in her hand, she twisted her body to watch his march across the room. "Indeed? And when, pray tell, would I have had the time to disclose any information about myself? If you remember, we had about three days from the time we were discovered in the library at the Ashbourne ball and our wedding. And after that, I was delirious with fever for days."

He waved the glass at her. "The hurried wedding was not my fault, I assure you. I had no intention of…"

"Of offering for me?" Her eyes snapped. "I know that, 'tis not a secret. And I asked you more than once to allow me to cry off."

Although it was no more Arabella's fault than it was his that they'd ended up married to each other, she still must learn to comport herself properly.

As he studied her, his body seemed to take notice of her appearance. Straggling curls fell about her face from her disheveled topknot, surrounding her flushed face. Her eyes were darkened, and she chewed on her lower lip. The last time he'd see her looking this way, she'd been underneath him, writhing with passion.

He drew in a calming breath, and trying to ignore what his body was doing, he placed the glass of whiskey on the table. "I doubt my feeble attempt at assistance will be of any service, but if it will help clear this mess up sooner, I will help."

He tamped down his annoyance when Arabella cast him a glowing smile. He almost preferred the feeling of suppressed passion to the knot of something soft that teased his insides at the beaming look on her face. Something he preferred not to think about.

"But don't let that cat near me." He growled to cover his confusion.

• • •

A small twinge of happiness brought a smile to Arabella's face. It appeared she'd won this battle. Of course, she was fully aware that countesses did not perform surgery. That was one of the reasons she'd eschewed marriage. She had wanted her freedom for as long as possible. As a young lady of the nobility, the only freedom afforded her was the choice of which gown to wear to a ball and which ribbon would match best.

"Here, Nash, hold this basket closer to the fire so I can see more clearly." She pointed to the brown basket with Cleopatra.

"I am beginning to itch already." He sneezed once. "It

might be a better idea to go closer to the window."

Arabella shook her head. "No, they need the warmth from the fire." She held up a needle and pushed the thread through as Nash slid the basket over and knelt alongside her.

He grabbed his handkerchief from his pocket, shook it out, and placed it over his nose. "Are you sure you know what you are doing?"

"I've done this many times. Now you will need to hold Cleopatra down while I sew her up, since this will hurt."

"Egad! I'll be sneezing until Christmastide morn. Why not give her a shot of whiskey to calm her down?"

Arabella sat back on her heels and studied him. "Whiskey? Why I have never thought of that. I tried laudanum once, but since I was afraid of using too much and killing Caesar—that was one of the squirrels I tended—I'm afraid it didn't do much, and I ended up getting bit. Thankfully, Sophia offered to hold him, so we got it done."

"And why, might I ask, is Sophia not here helping now?"

"She is packing. As you demanded, my lord." She smirked. "And, she might have been sick to her stomach for the rest of the day after the last time." Those words were mumbled, but nevertheless Nash snorted, so he must have heard them.

He rose. "I'll be right back. Anything to get this over with." He headed to the sideboard and picked up the small amount of whiskey he'd poured for himself. "Here." He handed the glass to her.

"You need to hold her head so I can pour it down her throat."

"She's bleeding!" He sneezed.

"Apparently, all this disturbance in your library has not diminished your ability to see and hear," she quipped.

"Arabella…"

"All right. I will hold her and you pour."

With very little trouble, they managed to get enough

of the whiskey down so that after about five minutes the cat was snoring. Arabella watched the cat's eyes close with amazement. "That worked quite well. You are an excellent surgeon's assistant."

Nash blew his nose and wiped his dripping eyes. "Not a role I intend to repeat. Let's dose the other one, so we can finish up."

After dosing Hercules, Nash tied his handkerchief around his nose and mouth and put on his leather gloves as he held one animal, then the other, while Arabella sewed. She wasn't quite sure since she was busy, but it sounded to her as though Nash gagged at one point.

"There." She sat back and admired her work. "All I need to do now is cover the wounds with a clean cloth and let them sleep." She grinned at him. "Thank you so much for your help. The whiskey was a wonderful idea."

Nash grunted and stood. "This needs to stop, Arabella. If you want to take up some type of hobby, try watercolors or embroidery. Or gardening. Something suitable to your station." He removed the handkerchief and used it to wipe his nose.

"Now you went and ruined it." She accepted his hand and rose. "I do not see why I cannot continue to help my animals. For heaven's sake, no one needs to know. Besides, Her Grace, the Duchess of Manchester conducts her botany experiments by digging in the dirt, and her husband not only allows it, but follows her about to help."

"Everyone is aware that Manchester allows his duchess to act in an unseemly manner because he is completely besotted with her."

As you will never be with me, nor I with you.

"If you will excuse me, my lord, I have a few items to take care of before I dress for dinner." Her back stiff, she swept past him and left the room.

"What about this mess in my library?"

She turned back to him with her hand on the door handle. "If a countess does not perform surgery, then certainly, a countess does not clean, my lord. I will have the maids see to it." With a little more enthusiasm than was warranted, she closed the library door just as Nash let out with a wholehearted sneeze.

Oh, the man absolutely infuriated her! She rounded the corner toward the stairs and practically ran her mother down. "Oh, Mother, you frightened me."

"Arabella, a lady does not rush about." She glared at her apron. "And what in heaven's name have you been up to now?"

"Two of my animals were injured. I had to sew them up."

Her mother actually paled. "What is the matter with you?" She spoke in a low, furious voice. "Your husband will not want his wife sewing up animals. You are a countess, now, Arabella. You must put these childish activities behind you. What would Lord Clarendon say if he saw you now?"

"I would say 'tis time she put these childish activities behind her." Nash strode down the corridor. "But now I suggest we all clean up and dress for dinner. We have an early start in the morning, so I asked Cook to move dinner up two hours earlier."

Well, who would ever imagine her husband and Mother not only agreeing on something, but both of them glaring at her as if she were a disobedient child. All of the fight went out of her. Despite what she had told everyone, her body was still weak from her illness. "If you will excuse me, I will order my bath."

Arabella turned to climb the stairs and stumbled as her knees weakened. Nash grabbed her around the waist and swung her into his arms. "We will see you at dinner, Lady Melrose." He proceeded to carry her up the stairs. Instead of protesting, she laid her head on his chest. She tried to fight the comfort she felt, but it was no use. She snuggled into his arms as he reached her door and bent to open the latch.

Once inside, he carried her to the bed and laid her gently down. "Perhaps a tray in your room would be best tonight." Her heart warmed at the look of concern on his face. He really was a nice man.

When he wasn't being arrogant and self-righteous.

"I am sure after a bath I will feel much better."

He studied her. "I think not. Call for Sophia and have her attend you, and I will join you after my bath. I will send word to your mother that we are dining here."

Although she knew it was not a good idea to allow him to order her about like that, truth be known, she was too tired to argue. "Yes. Perhaps that would be best."

He threw up his hands and raised his face to the ceiling. "Hallelujah. My wife agrees with me." His harsh words were softened by the indulgent look he gave her. Something deep inside her twisted, but she quickly squashed it.

Nash bent and kissed her on the forehead. "I will ring for Sophia and join you shortly."

Arabella was fast asleep when Sophia awoke her to help her into the bath. After a luxurious soak in lavender- and lemon-scented water, she climbed out of the tub and allowed Sophia to dry her off and dress her in another new nightgown, pale yellow with lace at the bodice and cuffs. Sophia left and Arabella slid into a matching wrapper just as Nash knocked and entered the room.

He wore a red and black striped banyan, his hair still damp from his bath. As he walked, the bottom of the dressing gown opened to reveal muscular calves covered with light brown hair. She had a hard time taking her eyes off his movements as his elegant feet drew him closer to her.

"Dinner will arrive momentarily." He took her hand,

kissing the skin with his warm lips. "You look lovely."

"I should really have checked on the animals—"

Irritation flashed across his face as he held up his hand. "No. No animals, no surgery, no blood. Tonight, we will enjoy a quiet dinner, an early bed, and then off to Suffolk in the morning."

She couldn't help but wonder if early to bed meant a repeat of last night's bed activities. Despite her fatigue, the thought of what they'd enjoyed the night before brought a flutter to her stomach. Before she had the opportunity to dwell on that, a scratch at the door announced the arrival of two footmen carrying dinner trays.

"Set them over there." Nash pointed to the table in the middle of the room with two chairs all ready for their use.

Once the men left, Nash held out her chair, and inhaling all the wonderful scents, she said, "Everything smells wonderful."

The display of fish soup, lamb chops, braised mushrooms, green peas, two jellies, a pudding, and fresh fruit reminded her how very hungry she was. Nash poured them both glasses of wine, and they began their dinner.

"Am I to trust you are all ready to leave first thing tomorrow morning?" Nash studied her over the top of his wine glass. "I do want to get an early start."

"Yes. Sophia has everything packed. I believe she had the footman take my trunk down to the carriage already."

He nodded. "Excellent."

Once they finished their meal, Nash poured himself a brandy and a sherry for her, and they retired to the two chairs in front of the fireplace. All the enthusiasm for bed activities had been wiped out by her fatigue, the heavy meal, and the sherry. When the room grew quiet, she found herself nodding off, until Nash stood and took the drooping glass from her hand.

"'Tis time for bed, sweeting." He took her hand and

walked her the short distance to the bed. He helped her remove her wrapper, then slipping off his banyan, joined her under the covers.

Tomorrow they would head to Suffolk. Arabella was anxious to see the manor, specifically where they would be able to build a larger kennel than the one in London. There should be plenty of room at a country estate for her to take in more animals. With that pleasant thought, she drifted off to sleep.

Chapter Eleven

Nash tapped his foot, waiting in the entrance hall for his wife to make an appearance. Once again, he checked his watch. He'd told Arabella he wished to leave at dawn. Here it was nearly eight o'clock, and she was still giving last-minute instructions on the care and feeding of her cursed animals.

It had taken quite a few lively discussions before he'd flat out ordered her to leave the animals behind. He had no intention of sneezing all the way to Suffolk if he had to share his ride with recovering animals. Nor would he allow another carriage to haul them all. With their vehicle, and the one for Sophia and Andrews with all their trunks, the entourage was extensive enough.

"Arabella." He strode down the corridor to the kitchen where she held court with two footmen and Cook. She waved her arms around, still explaining.

A quick glance at what he assumed was his exasperated face, she said, "I am ready, my lord." She stooped to give last-minute pats to the several animals in recuperation, then with a sad smile joined him. "Couldn't we at least take—"

"No." He grabbed her elbow and marched her down the corridor, out the door, down the steps, and into the carriage. He snatched her reticule from Quinn's hand as he passed by.

Arabella settled into the carriage and straightened her gown. "My goodness. Was it absolutely necessary for you to propel me out the door that way?"

"Yes. We would have been there another hour had I left it up to you to decide the time was right to leave those beasts."

"They are hardly beasts, and they need me."

"And I needed you to leave." He took a deep breath. "Let us not start off this trip at odds with each other."

"I agree." Arabella settled into her seat. "Tell me about Clarendon Manor."

He loved his home in Suffolk and enjoyed talking about it. "Except for when I was at school, I spent most of my life there until I took my seat in Parliament. The house actually dates back to the Elizabethan era. The exterior of the house retains that appearance, but most of the interior was remodeled over the years. The gardens were at one time extensive, but we have cut back on them since before my father's time."

"It sounds as though you enjoy time in the country."

"Yes. Mother did not approve of her children living in Town, felt the air was not good for our lungs. Consequently, Eugenia and I were left at the Manor oftentimes for months at a time with her governess, my tutor, and other staff members. Mother would visit us at least once a month for a week or more while she and Father were in London.

"Once I went off to Eton, and then University, Eugenia was left by herself with no playmates. Although, even when I was at home, she was forced to spend a great deal of time indoors while I was allowed much more freedom. Mother had strict rules for my sister."

"And for you?"

"Well, as a boy I wasn't forced to sit for hours and

embroider or do watercolors. Eugenia also spent a great deal of time practicing how to walk, how to sit. I think Mother even tied a board of some sort to her back to improve her posture."

"Good heavens. Poor Eugenia. It seems so unfair."

Nash shrugged. "I never questioned the discrepancy, since I was led to believe little girls had delicate constitutions and therefore could not run, play, or climb trees as well as little boys."

Arabella stared at him. "I don't believe that. Not for one moment. There is no doubt in my non-delicate mind that little girls can climb, run, and jump as well as little boys. I have done such myself, and should we have daughters, I expect them to have some freedom as well as learning their necessary lessons."

"I suppose you spent all of your girlhood taking care of stray animals."

"Not all of it. Like Eugenia, I had lessons in comportment, manners, watercolors, embroidery, and pianoforte. I also learned French and German, along with math, geography, and history. Father insisted that I have a well-rounded education.

"But, yes, as a matter of fact, I did spend too much time, according to Mother, rescuing animals and tending to their injuries. I loved when I could provide care for an animal that I found. Though my mother was and still is not too fond of my 'little hobby,' as she calls it.

"Speaking of Mother, not that she said so, but I think she is concerned that you are less than delighted with her and wish for her to stay out of your way for a while."

Nash shook his head. If that was the woman's concern, she certainly hadn't wasted any time in settling herself into his home. "Truthfully, I have not yet completely gotten over my angst at what she did. Not just to me, by accident, but to you. It angers me that she thought so little of your appeal that she felt it was necessary to foist you off on a man old enough to be your grandfather. However, she is your mother, and will receive the necessary respect from me, and my staff, as well.

"That being said, I own a house in Bath that I leave for my mother's use, or Eugenia's, if she desires to visit. If your mother wishes to have privacy, she is more than welcome to reside there. Or if she would like to holiday there."

Arabella stared at him. "Thank you. I will suggest it to her. She might like that very much, in fact. At one time, she visited Bath at least once a year. She still has friends there with whom she corresponds." Her whispered words, and the relief on her face, touched him.

He gave her a crooked smile. "Did you expect me to toss your mother out into the streets?"

"Well, since you seem quite anxious to do the same with my animal friends, the thought had crossed my mind." She smiled back, her eyes full of laughter.

He reached for her hand and slowly withdrew her glove, the silky material sliding over her skin. He placed a light kiss on her palm and looked up at her through the curls resting on his forehead. "I am not in the habit of abandoning ladies to their fates."

He turned her hand over and stroked his thumb over the soft, sensitive skin at her wrist. "Ah, my countess, perhaps when you get to know me better, you will find I am not the ogre you believe me to be."

Her breath whooshed from her lungs, which she attempted to hide with a cough. She shifted in her seat, obviously affected by his actions. "Yes, perhaps."

His soft laughter at her discomfort with his attentions brought a scowl to her face.

They made one stop for a late luncheon and to switch horses at the Bull and Bear Inn a little more than halfway to Clarendon Manor. Restless and anxious to be freed from the carriage, Nash was quite happy when he was able to note the beginning of Clarendon land, with only about a half-hour distance from the front door.

The sun had set, and it was near dark when the carriage rolled to a stop in front of his estate home. Since word had been sent ahead that their arrival was imminent, the household servants stood outside, lined up, awaiting their master and new mistress.

"I will introduce you to the staff, but since it grows dark, I suggest you refrain from too much conversation. You will have time over the next few days to speak more fully to them."

He climbed out and turned to help her down. She shook out her skirts and put a bright smile on her face as she linked her arm with his and they walked up the stone path and greeted the head butler, Morton.

Based on the dark circles under her eyes and the lines of fatigue on her face, it was apparent Arabella was exhausted from the trip, but she nevertheless showed the proper interest as Morton bowed to them both. After introductions were made, he proceeded down the line to introduce all the house male servants. His housekeeper, Mrs. Davies, then continued on and introduced all the female servants.

Arabella was gracious, charming, and unaffected. Truth be known, he was very proud of her at that moment. She had the correct balance of approachability without a suggestion of inappropriate friendliness. The staff seemed enthralled with her, and Nash was hard pressed not to admit the same feeling himself.

On the other hand, his mood dampened a bit at the extensive possibilities that presented themselves with access to more wild animals. More surgery. More arguments. He would need to find a way to keep his stubborn little wife busy. Perhaps more time spent in bed? He grinned at the thought.

They were escorted to their bedchambers, Mrs. Davies only taking a few minutes to point out to Arabella what she needed to know for the night. "Your lady's maid has been busy since her arrival arranging your things."

"Thank you, Mrs. Davies. I look forward to speaking with you tomorrow, when we have time together."

The housekeeper nodded and turned to Nash. "Will you be dining this evening, my lord? Cook has a fine meal prepared for you and your bride."

"That sounds wonderful, but I believe we would like a light supper sent up. Lady Clarendon is recovering from an illness and I am afraid all the travel has left her weary, and we will be retiring early this evening."

"Of course, my lord. I am sorry to hear that." She curtsied to them both and left the room.

Arabella untied her bonnet and tossed it on the bed. "Thank you, Nash. I really was not anxious to dress for a formal dinner tonight."

For once she did not naysay him on his orders for them both. He walked to her and tilted her chin up. "We tend not to be formal in the country and keep country hours, as well. But you do appear tired. Why don't you have Sophia arrange for a bath, and we can meet in the sitting room adjoining our bedchambers in say, an hour, for our meal?"

"Yes. That would be perfect."

He bent and placed his lips on hers. Despite her fatigue, she responded, leaving him wondering just how tired his wife was. As soon as supper was over, he intended to find out.

• • •

The next morning, Arabella awoke alone in her bed at Clarendon Manor. After a lovely bath and a quiet supper the night before, she'd nodded off as she sat across from Nash over the small table that had been set up in the sitting room for their meal. He'd scooped her up and carried her to her bedchamber, tucked her in, and kissed her on the forehead. Then, instead of joining her, he'd left to return to his own bedchamber. She hadn't seen him since.

They'd been man and wife a few weeks, and he'd only come to her once. Had he found her so unsatisfactory that he'd decided to forego what she'd been told was a man's favorite activity? Or did he, like so many in the *ton*, keep a mistress who satisfied his baser needs?

The thought bothered her. Not a jealous person by nature, even so, she had no desire to share her husband with another woman. Especially one who would be much more experienced than she. Then, a little voice of reason whispered that she'd been sick for most of their married life, and the last two nights she'd been so tired Nash had been forced to assist her to bed. If she intended to keep him away from other women's beds, she would do well to stop dropping her head into her dessert each evening.

"Good morning, my lady." Sophia pulled back the bed curtains and then moved to the window to open the drapes. Low-hung gray clouds covered the sky, just the sort of weather that enticed one to curl up with a fire, a cup of tea, and a good book. But Nash had said during their journey that he was anxious to visit the tenants.

From what he'd told her, his steward, Mr. Jones, had been reporting less profits over the past couple of years than what they'd received for years before that. He had also claimed expenses had risen. When she questioned him, Nash admitted the thought had crossed his mind that Mr. Jones might be pilfering money from him, but he was an older man who had been employed by the Clarendon title for many years, as well as his father before him. It hardly seemed likely that he would suddenly begin to steal from them.

Arabella climbed from bed and allowed Sophia to tend to her morning ablutions. With a blue and white striped day dress and her hair in a sensible braid that Sophia had wrapped around her head, Arabella descended the stairs to the breakfast room. She'd been so tired the night before, she'd forgotten where Mrs. Davies had said it was and had to have a footman direct her.

Nash sat at the table, his newspaper covering his face. As soon as she entered, he placed the paper next to his plate and stood. "Good morning. You had a restful sleep, I assume?"

"Yes, I did. I hardly remember finishing our supper last evening."

"You were a bit weary, but I must say, you look quite refreshed this morning."

Did the twinkle in his eye and lopsided smile mean he intended to play the husband tonight? A shiver ran through her at the thought of his warm, large hands on her naked flesh. Yes, she was ready for another go at playing wife.

"I would like to make the first rounds of tenant visits in about an hour. There are several I wish to speak with about this drop in production Mr. Jones keeps sending correspondence about. Before you came down, I took a short ride to the closest farms and saw no evidence of such. That disturbs me for more than one reason. I do not like employing someone whose trust I question, and it reminds me that I have been neglecting my estate duties in favor of Parliament."

He took a sip of coffee from his blue and white china cup and placed it back into the saucer. "Will you be ready?

She studied him as he spoke. His country dress was less formal than Town dress. His beige breeches, tucked into shiny Hessian boots, fit snugly over his bulging muscles. He wore no waistcoat under his dark green woolen jacket. A loosely tied cravat, giving him a somewhat rakish look, completed the outfit. The man was definitely not hard to look at. The heat rose once again in her face. "Yes, I will be ready as soon as I finish breakfast."

"Excellent." He stood and pushed his chair back. "I wish to go over the correspondence I brought with me from London, so when you are ready, please join me in the library. If you don't remember where that is, just ask one of the footmen to direct you." Kissing her on the top of her head, he quit the room.

Arabella took her time eating her breakfast since Nash had given her an hour. She idly looked over the newspaper. Since it had arrived by post, it bore the previous day's date. As she leisurely turned the pages, she took only a quick glance at the Society pages. She'd never been interested in who was intending to offer for whom, who the new Incomparable was, and which debutante was not receiving enough attention, despite her large dowry. She shook her head at the nonsense she was so happy to be away from. Perhaps they could spend the rest of the Season in the country.

She finished her breakfast and took a slow walk to her bedchamber to retrieve her bonnet and gloves.

Her new home was a bit different from the home in which she'd been raised. Clarendon Manor boasted thick carpets, silk wall coverings, and old, but well-cared-for, furniture. While her childhood homes had been quite pleasant, this one spoke of a family with perhaps more funds to keep it up to standard.

She hoped to have time during the day to take a tour with Mrs. Davies, but now she needed to present herself to Nash for their tenant visits. Drawing on her gloves, she checked her appearance in the mirror and followed a footman to the library.

Nash sat behind an immense desk, an open ledger book in front of him, his hands propping his head up. From the condition of his hair, he must have spent some time running his fingers through it.

"Are things bad?" She took the chair in front of his desk.

In her entire life, she had never given money a thought. She'd visited the shops along Bond Street and had the bills sent to Father. Only once had Mother mentioned that perhaps Arabella could do without a gown she had desperately wanted for an upcoming ball. That had been the first time money, or perhaps a lack thereof, had ever been brought to her attention.

"I'm sure my dowry can be put to good use. I know Papa always said it was a significant amount. I assume that will help?"

Chapter Twelve

I assume that will help?

Nash studied Arabella. Apparently, her mother had not told her about dipping into her dowry to keep them both from starving after the late earl had cocked up his toes. But, since Nash had hidden their situation from *his* mother, he felt no obligation to tell his wife, either. Women were to be protected. It was his duty to provide for all the women in his life. Arabella, Mother, and now, his mother-in-law. He would get to the bottom of the lack of funds, and hopefully, the investment he hoped to join would help. Until then, it was his problem to deal with and solve.

"Everything is fine, my dear. You are not to trouble yourself." He slammed the ledger book closed and stood. "Now I would like to take my wife on a round of calls to the tenants so they can meet you. Cook has put together baskets that we will bring with us. It is a family tradition. If they are all prepared, have one of the footmen load them into the carriage. I will make sure the correct carriage has been brought around."

"How many will we be visiting?"

"We will try perhaps four or five today. More tomorrow." He rounded the desk and took her arm. "I like your gown. It suits you." He studied her head. "And your hair. You look very much the lord of the manor's wife."

Blushing prettily, she gave him a slight curtsy. "Thank you, my lord."

Life could be quite pleasant when they weren't at odds with each other. One place his wife was quite amenable was the bedchamber. That was where her incongruous behavior was quite acceptable. He also saw in her a desire to try new things. His blood warmed and traveled south at all the new things he could offer to show her.

He intended to make love to his wife tonight. Two nights of tucking her into bed with no more than a peck on her forehead were beginning to wear on him. In the time they'd been married, he'd only had the pleasure of her body once. Frustrated last evening when she had again fallen asleep at the table, he'd left her and retired to his chamber, alone.

After which he had doused his frustration with a few snifters of brandy. That was not a habit he intended to continue. He needed the release of a woman's body and intended to have her as much as he wanted.

He'd dismissed his mistress shortly after he'd announced his betrothal to Arabella at Ashbourne's ball. Loyalty meant a great deal to him, and he felt his wife deserved his loyalty, just as he fully expected the same from her. He would not tolerate taking lovers even once an heir and a spare had made their appearances.

The thought of Arabella lying in the arms of another man twisted his insides. Not that he was jealous. It was just that she was his and his alone. Nor did he intend to fall in love. That had never been his intention, no matter who he married. Love made for misunderstandings and hurt feelings. In addition to poor Wentworth, he'd seen other besotted husbands act in such crazed ways that he never wanted to be counted among their numbers. He'd always had an abhorrence of appearing foolish.

Nash was discussing the mixture they used for feed for his horses with one of the grooms when Arabella joined him. A footman carrying the baskets followed behind. Once again, he observed her as she instructed the servant where to place the food inside the wagon. She did, indeed, present herself as the perfect picture of a noble's wife. Off to visit the tenants and offer advice and food items.

Her blue bonnet didn't hide the front of her hair where the tight braids were fastened, the golden-brown locks woven into an intricate pattern. Even in the dull gray of the low-hanging clouds, Nash felt her presence like sunshine. Her smile was genuine, and warmth from her happy demeanor spread through his insides.

"Are we ready?" The excitement in her voice brought a smile to his face, and a sense of adventure. Never before had he so looked forward to tenant visits. Of course, given how little time he'd spent at the Manor since he'd gained his title, tenant visits had fallen off since his father's death.

"Yes. We are all ready." He helped Arabella into the carriage and followed her in. With the baskets piled on one of the benches, they sat together on the other bench. He took her hand in his and intertwined their fingers as the carriage rolled away from the manor and headed toward Mr. and Mrs. Blossom's house, the closest cottage. Arabella turned to him. "Tell me about the first tenants we're to visit."

Nash rested his booted foot on his bent knee. "Harold Blossom and his wife, Emma, have four children. They occupy what used to be his parents' home and adjoining farm. Old Ned Blossom passed on a few years ago. Up until his death, he kept his finger in their farm operation, giving Harold a lot of advice." He grinned. "Some of it even wanted, I imagine.

"Harold and I, along with some of the other lads, spent our summers swimming in the pond—that is, when I could dodge my tutor."

Arabella appeared shocked. "Your parents allowed you to play with the tenants' children?"

Nash nodded and pointed out the window. "There is the Blossom farm." Neat rows of oats and rye stretched from the back of the house and out a few acres. A small garden that supplied the large family with vegetables and herbs sat alongside the east side of the house. Mrs. Blossom had used the front area of the farmhouse to plant flowers. Even with four children to tend to, the house and yard were well kept.

Nash stepped from the carriage and assisted Arabella just as Blossom and his wife approached them, bright welcoming smiles on their faces. Mrs. Blossom carried a baby on her hip and another little one attached to her skirts. Harold stuck his hand out. "My lord. I can't tell you how good it is to see you."

Not standing on ceremony with these longtime tenants, Nash took the farmer's hand and they shook. "'Tis good to see you, as well, Blossom. It's been far too long."

"Yes, it has." Harold motioned with his chin toward his wife. "We have two new little ones since you last visited."

Nash felt the stabbing guilt at having neglected the responsibilities to his estate. He had soothed his conscience by telling himself his duties to Parliament took precedence. Standing here with this hardworking farmer, looking at the land worked by the man's family for generations, brought the realization that he had been quite mistaken. If, indeed, there were shenanigans going on with Jones, he truly had no one to blame but himself. He vowed again to make sure he spent more time in Suffolk, seeing to his obligations.

Nash turned toward Arabella. "I would like to make known to you Mr. Harold Blossom and his wife, Mrs. Emma

Blossom. Their family has lived here for generations." He took her hand and pulled her forward. "This is my wife, her ladyship, the Countess of Clarendon."

Arabella smiled at the couple. The man tugged on the brim of his hat, and the woman did a quick dip.

"Oh my lady, 'tis a true pleasure to meet you." Mrs. Blossom smiled brightly at Arabella. "We were so thrilled when word reached us that the master had married." She looked toward Nash. "I hope that means we will be seeing more of you, my lord."

"That is my full intention, Mrs. Blossom. I am afraid I have been somewhat neglectful since my father's passing. That will soon change."

"We brought your family a little something from our cook." Arabella held out the basket to Mrs. Blossom. "I hope you enjoy her efforts."

The woman's cheeks grew rosy. "Thank you so much, my lady. I am sure we will."

• • •

Arabella knelt to the ground and spoke to the little girl clinging to her mother's skirts. "Hello, little one. What is your name?"

The girl twisted her tiny hand in her mother's skirts and tugged them forward to cover her face.

"I'm so sorry, my lady," the mother said. "She's a shy one, this one. Her name is Dorothy." She tapped the little girl on the head. "Remember your manners. Say hello to Lady Clarendon."

Dorothy shook her head back and forth and stuck her little thumb into her mouth, continuing to stare at Arabella with wide chocolate-brown eyes.

"That is all right, Mrs. Blossom. I understand. I was quite

shy as a child, myself." Arabella rose.

"Oh dear me. Here I am, scolding my Dorothy for poor manners, and I am leaving you to stand out here. Please come inside and have some tea. I just finished baking some biscuits." Mrs. Blossom led the way for them all to enter the house.

It was a small cottage, smelling of sugar and spices. Probably from the biscuits she'd just baked. Two little boys sat at a table, sharing a worn book. One was reading aloud with corrections made by his brother. The house was warm and comfortable. Mrs. Blossom had made a cozy home for her family. Arabella was amazed at what the family had done with the limited resources they had available to them.

Arabella took a seat near the two boys and read along with them while still conversing with Mrs. Blossom. Nash discussed farm matters with the husband, his eyebrows pulled together in a frown at some of the information the farmer gave him. After about twenty minutes, Nash nodded at Arabella and stood. "I'm afraid as much as I am enjoying our conversation, Lady Clarendon and I have other calls to make."

The couple walked with them to the carriage. Just as they were saying their final good-byes, one of the boys raced from the small house shouting for his father. Blossom grabbed the boy by the shoulders. "Whoa there, son. What is all the shouting about?"

"You must come, Papa. Daisy has Bessie trapped in the corner and is about to eat her!"

"Excuse us, my lord, but it appears my boy's pet is in danger."

Before he took two steps a wired-hair dog raced from the house with a small animal in its jaws. "Papa, look!" The child pointed and jumped up and down frantically.

The dog sprinted past them and huddled next to the carriage wheel, watching the humans with narrowed eyes. The small white kitten anchored between its teeth squealed and wiggled its body.

Arabella looked at the little boy. "Is that your pet there in the dog's mouth?"

"Yes, my lady. That is Booker." He wiped his eyes with his sleeve. "And Daisy's about to eat him."

"How many times have I told you to keep that kitten in the cage and away from that dog?" Mrs. Blossom wrapped her arms around her son's shoulders.

Arabella walked toward the dog, murmuring to the animal. The dog hunkered down, its tail moving back and forth as it watched her approach. "You don't want to hurt that little kitty, do you, Daisy?" She got down on her knees and reached out, petting the dog. After a few minutes the dog laid down. Arabella reached out and rubbed the animal's stomach, murmuring until she scratched under the dog's chin, and he opened his jaw, dropping the kitten, who scooted away.

The little boy ran up with a box, and the kitten darted into it.

Beaming, Arabella climbed to her feet and walked back to where the adults stood. Mrs. Blossom thanked her profusely, but Nash glowered at her, wiping the smile from her face.

"It is time to go." He grabbed her elbow and practically shoved her into the carriage. Once they were side-by-side on the padded bench, Arabella wrenched her elbow free. "Whatever is the matter with you?"

"How many times do I have to tell you that countesses do not crawl around in the dirt and rescue animals? You forget your position."

"My position just now was to save the pet for that little boy. Did you not see his tears?"

"They could certainly have rescued the animal without your help." He looked at her knees in disgust. "Brush your skirt. It's full of dirt."

Indeed, her gown was dirty. With quick movements, she

brushed the dirt off and stared out the window. The man was insufferable!

After a while, Arabella's anger had lessened and she took a deep breath. "I am sorry you were disappointed in me, but I felt the need to help the little boy."

Nash waved away her comments. "Just don't ever do that again."

She swallowed her angry retort and decided to make peace. "How did your conversation with Mr. Blossom go?" She grabbed the strap alongside her head as the carriage hit rough ground.

"Confusing."

Her raised eyebrows brought more information. "Mr. Blossom claims he has not been having poor crops or other issues that my steward had informed me the tenants were dealing with. He also mentioned something about the rent on his farm going up, and I never requested an increase in rent."

"Sounds suspicious to me," Arabella said.

Nash nodded. "Rather than jump to any conclusions, I will talk with the other tenants and see what they have to say before I approach Jones. That is, if I am able to locate the man. He has not answered my summons. Did you enjoy your time with Mrs. Blossom?"

"Yes. She is a lovely woman. Her two sons were teaching each other to read. One was a level above the other, but he was still learning new words himself. I assume they are needed to work the farm, but is there a school they attend?"

"No. The parents do the teaching. Naturally, some better than others, but one or two of the tenants' lads showed some promise, and the local rector took it upon himself to continue their instruction once they surpassed what their parents had to offer."

"I would love to see the day when all children may attend school on a regular basis."

"Ah, I think I hear rumblings of rebellion from my countess. Are you favoring the Whigs, then?" He winked at her.

"Perhaps." She gave him a saucy smile. "Would that put us at odds once again?"

He reached out and tucked a curl back into her bonnet. "More than we are now?"

"And here I thought we were getting on so famously." When all was well, and there was no bickering about her animals or his expectations for her, she loved these little repartees they shared.

Nash leaned forward and murmured in her ear. "I look forward to us getting along quite well later this evening." Before she could offer a retort, he cupped her chin in his hand and covered her lips with his warm, soft ones. She sighed with contentment, happy to once again feel the tingles in various places in her body at her husband's touch.

Nash pulled away and tapped her on the edge of her nose. "Later." He glanced over her shoulder and pointed. "Coming up is the Fernside farm. As a boy, I played with their two sons, as well."

Still under the spell of his kiss, it took Arabella a moment to compose herself. Then she twisted in her seat to see a stone cottage with fields of grain behind it.

Nash continued as he rubbed the soft skin at the back of her neck with his finger and thumb. Honestly, if the man did not stop touching her this way, she would become a bumbling idiot. Then who would be to blame if she made an arse of herself with his tenants?

The carriage came to a rolling stop in front of the small, but tidy, farm. Arabella once again noticed very well-tended crops and family gardens. Whatever issues Nash's steward was grumbling about hadn't become noticeable as of yet.

The older couple waited at their front door and greeted

Nash and Arabella with smiles, as well. It seemed as if Nash was truly beloved by his tenants. That was very comforting.

"Well, hello there, my lord. I was hoping you would see your way here. We heard yesterday that you were expected and would be bringing your new bride." Mr. Fernside limped slightly as he moved forward, his wife beside him.

"Hello to you, Fernside." He turned to Arabella. "This is Mr. and Mrs. Fernside. They are valued tenants, and their family has been with us for generations."

"It seems to me sometimes, my lord, that I, myself, have been here for generations." Fernside tugged on the brim of his cap and nodded at Arabella. "My lady."

Mrs. Fernside offered a slight dip and fussed with her apron, her cheerful face flushing as she spoke. "May I ask you to honor us with a visit inside, my lord, my lady? Since I was hoping you would be by, I made my special apple cake."

Nash took the basket out of Arabella's hands and holding onto her elbow, moved her forward. "We are in for a real treat if Mrs. Fernside made her famous apple cake. Their two sons, David and Michael, would swipe it from the windowsill while it was cooling, and we all three would devour it."

Mrs. Fernside wagged her finger. "Ah, but what you didn't know, my lord, was I always made two. One I put up high so the lads couldn't find it."

"See, she was on to our tricks," Nash said, winking at Arabella.

Another comfortable home, this one was quieter, with no children around. "I have lost touch the last couple of years. Where are Michael and David?" Nash settled himself in a chair at the wooden table as Mrs. Fernside placed dishes and a teapot on the table.

"Michael married a little gel from Essex. Moved to her family's farm. David took himself off to the American Colonies."

"So, you work the place yourself?"

"We cut back a bit, and once in a while my nephew comes by to help. It would be all right if it weren't for the raise in rent." Fernside ducked his head and blushed, obviously regretting complaining about a raise to the landlord.

Nash crossed his arms over his chest and leaned back in his chair. "Tell me about this raise, Mr. Fernside."

The tenant visits continued for the rest of the afternoon. By the time Nash and Arabella waved good-bye to the last farm on their list, Arabella was exhausted. Who would have thought playing lord and lady of the manor could be so tiring? And truth be known, any weight she'd lost with her illness had truly come back today with all the biscuits, cakes, and tarts they'd been offered.

Each family had been more welcoming than the one before. She found it a satisfying experience to visit tenants. Something she would certainly enjoy, along with caring for animals. Yes, life at Clarendon Manor could be quite pleasant. But first, she must get through the Season in London and Nash's demands that she take on her role as his countess with the *ton's* approval.

Once the carriage began its journey toward home, Nash placed his arm around her shoulders and pulled her close to his side. His large hand cupped her chin and turned her face up to him. Slowly, his head descended, his lips taking hers in a possessive kiss. His tongue slid along the seam of her lips until his nudging encouraged her to open her mouth. They parried and sucked and then he swept over her teeth, and her lower lip, where he stopped to nip, then soothe the soft skin. "I suggest we again have an informal dinner in your room when we return home." He spoke against her lips, his voice deeper, huskier.

"It looks as though we will never use the dining room, my lord." Goodness, her voice didn't sound much better.

"I can think of many ways to use the dining room table," he said. "None of them require food, however."

Had he meant what she thought he'd meant? She looked up at him and then sucked in a breath at the smirk on his handsome face. "Surely, you don't mean—"

"Yes, I do." He leaned his head close to her ear, his voice lowered to a pitch that had her wanting to remove their clothes and feel him skin-to-skin. "There are also the many carpets, the chairs, the library desk, the settee, the gazebo."

She drew back. "Outside!"

"Why not?"

The man was downright wicked, but a kernel of excitement grew in her lower parts at the vision of them naked in the outdoors.

"What I am wanting is an intimate dinner with my lovely wife, and delectable ways to spend the time after dinner." He grinned. "Consider it dessert."

Arabella gazed up at him, already lost in his spell. Thinking of the road dust and hours spent in the carriage, she said, "Yes, I believe that would be a good idea, though I would like a bath first."

He bowed his head. "As you wish."

Arabella's heart thundered at this point. Excitement shot through her, and she could already feel herself damp between her legs.

As if he sensed her thoughts, Nash once again placed his mouth near her ear and ran his tongue over the soft shell. "Have no fear, Arabella. We will take our time. We have all night."

Oh dear.

Chapter Thirteen

Nash knocked lightly on Arabella's bedchamber door. He'd given her enough time to bathe and prepare herself. He was looking forward to a night spent in his wife's bed with her naked curves plastered against him in sleep.

Today had been particularly satisfying, despite Arabella's faux pas with the animals at Blossom's farm. He shook his head, considering how her behavior would have been viewed had a member of Polite Society been present. On the other hand, Blossom and his wife had been grateful for her assistance and had not seemed to think any less of her for her actions.

Otherwise, she'd made an excellent impression on his tenants, and the staff already turned to her for instructions, which removed a great deal of burdensome decisions from his shoulders.

Thinking of his tenants raised his ire again at the condition of his finances. He'd learned from one of his tenants that his steward, Edward Jones, had not been around to collect the rents for some time. It seemed his son, Randall Jones, had been collecting them on his father's behalf. Randall had told the tenants that his father was ill and he was helping. A trip to the Jones cottage had shown it locked up tight.

He pushed all of that aside at Arabella's response and opened the door. She stood there, all pink and glowing from her bath, in a thin cotton nightgown, her curves visible through the candlelight. The gown's bodice was low enough that the creamy mounds of her breasts rose and fell as she took in breaths. Her hair had been brushed to a gleaming mass of locks draped over her shoulders. She smiled softly at him. He continued his perusal of her body then glanced down at her hands.

She held a furry scrap of some sort of animal in her clutches. Blood dripped onto her pristine white night gown. And the rug. And the counterpane. And her tiny toes peeking out from under the gown.

"What the devil is that, Arabella?"

"I'm sorry, my lord, but one of the maids just brought him to me. He's been injured and needs my attention."

"*I* need your attention. We are not going to perform surgery again. I will ring for a footman who will take that— animal—to the kitchen and have Cook serve it up for breakfast."

She gasped and clutched the animal to her chest, then swung around, her back facing him, protecting the creature. "No. He is only a little kitten. We can't eat him for breakfast!"

"I insist. Well, not about eating the thing since I don't fancy kitten stew, but you will have a footman take it to the kitchen and have one of the maids clean it up." He raised his hand as she opened her mouth to speak. "That is my final word on this, Arabella." He walked to the bell rope and tugged.

She continued to pet and murmur to the kitten about the mean man while they waited. Ordinarily her soothing way with the kitten would have blood pumping to his groin, imagining her stroking him instead of the animal. However, the sight of all that blood and the animal's wails hindered any lustful thoughts.

A footman arrived, his eyebrows reaching his hairline when Nash had Arabella place the kitten in his hands. "Please see that one of the maids attends the kitten."

"Yes, my lord." He swallowed a few times. "And then what would you like us to do with it?"

Arabella shook her head furiously. No, he wouldn't tell the man to have it cooked up. "Just find a basket or something for it to sleep in for the night." He glanced over at Arabella. "And please have another bath sent up for her ladyship."

Nash sipped on a glass of brandy in his room, trying very hard not to listen to Arabella in her bath. So far, he had not succeeded. He would read a few lines, then picture her naked body in the warm, scented water, beaded liquid sliding ever so slowly over her flushed skin.

He slammed the book shut, tossed down the rest of his drink and decided she'd had long enough to wash off a bit of blood. Determined to hurry her up even if she were still bathing, he strode across the room and entered her bedchamber, coming to an abrupt stop.

She faced away from him and apparently hadn't heard him enter. Her hair was piled on top of her head, with strands of damp curls falling down the back of her neck. The creamy skin of her shoulders rose about the rim of the tub, urging him to place his lips there and taste the dampness of her flesh. She hummed softly, stroking her skin with a cloth.

He moved to the bathtub and knelt behind her. Her body stilled as he gave in to his urge and kissed her gently on her neck. She regarded him over her shoulder. "My lord? I am not finished."

"I know." He reached out and took the cloth from her hand and rubbed it with the lavender and lemon scented soap floating in the water. Pushing up his sleeves, he dipped the cloth into the water and smoothed it over her breasts. Her nipples immediately tightened and drew into two pouting beads. Her welcoming moan spurred him further, to nibble on her ear and lick the soft shell.

Arabella tilted her head to one side, and he dropped the cloth and used his fingertips to stroke her nipples before cupping them in his hands, kneading the flesh, feeling their weight. "Open your legs," he whispered. She did as he commanded, her bent knees resting against the sides of the tub.

A whispered "yes" escaped her lips as his fingers slid between her ebony curls, caressing, stroking, petting, much as she had cooed at the kitten. "Do you grow cold, sweetheart? The water is no longer warm."

When she turned her head to answer, he took her lips in a deep kiss, his fingers still fondling her intimate parts. His thumb circled and pressed against the jutting flesh that would bring her pleasure and eventually cause her to break apart in his arms.

Arabella whimpered when he withdrew his hands from the water. He moved to the chair next to the wall and scooped up a drying cloth Sophia had left there. "Stand," he said, his voice raspy as he returned to the tub.

Her eyes grew wide. "Stand?"

"Yes." He barely got the word out, his body so filled with lust he didn't think he could manage a complete sentence.

Like a nymph rising from the sea, Arabella stood, water dripping off every curve, running down her legs, beading on her nipples. He sucked in a breath, holding the cloth, but did not wrap her in it, his eyes feasting on the sight. "You are stunningly beautiful." The finest paintings in the Louvre did not compare to the beauty of this flesh and blood woman with curves and dips to tempt the most stalwart of saints.

Her soft laughter had his blood racing right to his cock. Before she could cover her luscious body, he extended his hand to help her out of the tub. Her flesh was pink from the bath, her dampened skin glowing. She took his hand, staring at him the entire time, her eyes never leaving his. Her breathing increased, her sweet breasts rising and falling, a sure sign she was affected by him watching her.

Gently, he dried her soft skin, taking his time, stopping at different points to caress, stroke, and fondle. She stood like a statue until he dropped the cloth and took her hands, placing them on his shoulders. He leaned in, the soft scent of her breath bathing his face. "I want you so much, my entire body aches."

"As does mine." She cast a siren's smile and wrapping her hands around his head, drew him closer, kissing him softly, until he could no longer stand the gentleness of her kiss. Pulling her flush against his body, he covered her mouth with his, nudging her lips until she opened, then swept his tongue in, loving the taste of tea and mint on her breath.

An overwhelming sense of possession flooded him, almost bringing him to his knees.

Mine. Only mine.

Never in his life, with any of the voluptuous and skilled mistresses and courtesans he'd slept with, had he felt this sense of the right woman being in his arms. She fit him like a well-made leather glove. Her soft curves melted into his hard planes. He loved her silky skin, the scent that came from her hair, the mewing sounds she made when he touched her intimately. When he looked into her eyes, he felt as though he were drowning.

Her innocent, but enthusiastic, response to his touches fired his blood. Nash scooped Arabella up, striding to the bed where he laid her gently and after shrugging out of his banyan, brought his body down on top of hers.

His hand stroked her from her slender shoulders to the dark curls at the apex of her thighs. His fingers nudged her until she opened her legs wider. A low moan rose from her lips when his fingers delved into her moistness and warmth, circling, rubbing. "Do you like that, sweetheart?"

"Yes." She drew the word out until it became a moan. Nash's lips covered the nipple on her plump breast and suckled, pulling and tugging until Arabella began thrashing her head back and forth, her breath coming in gasps. "Please, Nash. Please. Do something."

"What do you want, sweeting?" he whispered in her ear, his fingers busy at the entrance to her body, pushing in and out, stroking the swollen, damp part of her that would give her the pleasure every woman deserved. He gazed down at her face. She bit her lower lip, frowning in concentration as she attempted to reach the pinnacle he knew she longed for. That only he would ever give her.

"I want this agony to stop. I want…"

"I know what you want, my love. And I shall give it to you. Just relax, do not try so hard. When you fall, I will be here to catch you." He kissed her closed eyes, her nose, jaw, then moved down to suckle on her breast once more. When she continued to strain, he moved farther down, kissing her flushed skin, covering her belly with feather kisses and slight nips. Placing his hands under her buttocks, he lifted and placed his mouth where his fingers had been and stroked her moist opening with his tongue.

Honey. She tasted like honey, and he could not get enough.

"Yes, yes. That." Her breathing increased, and she fisted the sheets, calling his name over and over. Keeping his mouth busy, he looked up her thrashing body as a slight smile began on her lips, and then she stiffened, and a low keening erupted from deep inside as her body shuddered. He continued his ministrations until she collapsed, struggling to draw in breath.

As he watched her, something inside of him shifted. Something he did not want to identify. Instead, he kissed his way up her replete body and braced on his elbows, leaned over her, and looked into her hazel eyes.

All his past lovers had been merely practice for this one. This woman, in this time and place. He was home.

• • •

Arabella tried desperately to drag air into her lungs, but her chest heaved as though she'd run a race. She opened her eyes to see Nash staring at her, a definite look of male satisfaction on his face.

His warm lips covered hers, almost with violence, and she tentatively reached out for his jutting manhood. Would he be shocked and dismayed at her forwardness if she touched him? Would he tell her that was not what a countess did? He had seemed to enjoy her attentions there the last time they'd made love.

Her palm slid over his chest, tugging lightly on the soft curls that ran down the center to gather around the area she most wanted to explore. She continued on until she reached his hardened shaft. Nash sucked in a breath as her fingertips touched the incredibly soft skin covering steel. "Do you not want me to touch you there? I did the last time, but I don't want to shock you."

He smiled and held firmly onto her hand. "Do not be concerned with shocking me, darling. Anything we do here in our bed is fine as long as we both agree. And, yes, I definitely want you to touch me there."

The grimace on his face as she slowly moved her hand over the oddly shaped member, and then encircled it with her fingers, made her think he felt pain. "Are you sure this doesn't hurt?"

A groan was his only answer before he took her face in his two hands and devoured her mouth. He nudged her lips and his tongue slid in, tangling with hers, then sweeping over the inside of her mouth. The tingling that she'd felt before started up again, and her breathing once more increased.

"That's it, darling, keep doing just that."

The words he'd uttered were endearing, names he rarely used. Perhaps men had to be in the throes of passion before they spoke such tender words. How many women had Nash called darling, sweetheart, or sweeting? A depressing thought she shoved from her mind.

Her fingers slid into his thick curls, tugging his mouth once again to hers. She could not get enough of his skilled kisses. His hard body that pressed against hers still didn't seem close enough. She felt as though she wanted to burrow into him, become part of him.

"Sweetheart, I can't keep holding off. I'm sorry." He pulled back, then spread her legs with his knee, settling his muscular body between them. He continued his kisses and squeezing and molding her breasts. Slowly, the hardened part of him nudged at her center, and he moved into her, pulling out, then moving back in. It didn't hurt as much as it had the first time, just a feeling of fullness.

"Oh God, you feel wonderful. So tight, so warm and moist."

By the look on his face, that was either the worst thing in the world, or the best. He fully entered her, so their bodies touched, then he began moving. The rhythm grew from enjoyable to once again frantic as she shifted so the part of her that needed attention could rub against his manhood.

Nash leaned down to mumble in her ear, "Yes, keep moving like that. I love the feel of you underneath me. Your softness against my hardness."

Although she needed no encouragement, his words

spurred her on, making her feel as though she were a wanton. A woman who enjoyed her husband's attentions, unlike what Mother had told her. "Doing one's duty" was just that, a duty. Yet this was certainly no duty. This was wonderful.

As she moved, the warm feelings once again started to build as Nash thrust into her, again taking her breath away.

She sighed with delight, then licked his flat nipple, causing him to suck in a deep breath through his teeth.

He grabbed her hands and pulled them over her head. Holding them both with one large hand, he used the other one to massage her breast, tweak her nipple, his hips moving in rhythm. The roughness of his palm over the softness of her skin abraded her nipples, causing heaviness in her breasts and more moisture to gather between her legs.

"You make me crazy, Arabella," Nash whispered in her ear. "You are so warm, so soft. I can't get enough of you."

His muscled body, and the grip he had on her hands, anchoring her to the bed, excited her like nothing he'd done before. She looked up at him, and he stared at her, his blue eyes almost black. Blond curls fell over his forehead, urging her to brush them back, but he still held her hands.

She wanted so badly to touch him, but he held firm as he bent his head and took her mouth in a kiss that demanded her surrender. He nudged at her lips, and his tongue swept in. They tangled together, her desire to feel that wonderful sensation again rising with each stroke of his tongue.

"Oh God, sweetheart, I can't wait any longer." His voice was hoarse, raspy. Just as that delightful feeling started to wash over her, Nash threw his head back and shoved one last time. Warm liquid flooded her insides, but she barely noticed since she was again riding a wave of her own pleasure.

Nash collapsed on top of her, having as much trouble breathing as she was. After a few minutes of them both gasping for breath, he brushed back the damp curls from her forehead and kissed the spot he uncovered. "I hope I did not hurt you."

"No." She shook her head, her voice barely audible as she attempted to catch her breath.

"Good. I am afraid I was a tad eager from staying away from you, so you could sufficiently recover from your fatigue."

Nash rolled off her and pulled her to his side. They lay together, both of them regaining their breath. The silence was comforting until she began to feel chilly. When she shivered, Nash reached down and pulled the counterpane over them, pulling her even closer against him to share his incredible warmth. He seemed to be settling in for the night.

Almost as if he'd read her mind, he said, "I had always planned to share a bed with my wife." He looked down at her. "Do you object to that?"

Another surprise. Although he'd slept with her in the short time they'd been married, she'd assumed it was because of her illness. Had she given it thought, it would have surprised her that he wanted her by his side all night. Typical *ton* married couples had separate bedchambers. And beds. Indeed, the thought of curling up against Nash's warm body in the cold nights of winter sounded appealing.

"No." She shook her head. "I do not object at all."

He kissed her forehead again. "Good." His fingers drew lazy circles on her arm.

Weariness settled into her bones. "I believe I would like to sleep now. It has been a long day." She stifled a yawn and boldly kissed him on the lips and turned her back to him, snuggling into the covers.

A strong arm came around her waist and pulled her to his body. She rather liked having him next to her in bed. She wiggled her bottom a bit to settle against him, and he moaned.

She looked over her shoulder. "Does that hurt?"

"No, Arabella. Just go to sleep."

Chapter Fourteen

"How are my animals?" Nash groaned at the first words out of Arabella's mouth when they entered Clarendon Townhouse. They had stayed overnight at the Duck and Swan Inn, which had left them with only three hours on the road that morning. He had pushed Arabella to rise before dawn to finish their journey. He'd been anxious to get started on his finances.

After visiting with other tenants, he had determined his money problems were easily solved by hiring a new steward.

The younger Jones had never been located, but after confirming his suspicions, he had notified the magistrate to hold him when found. He also passed the word to all tenants that there would be a new steward, and they were no longer to deal with Jones. Once he settled his affairs in London, he would go back to Suffolk and meet with the tenants as a group and get all matters, including the so-called rent increase, straightened out.

"I believe one of the footmen has been caring for them, my lady." Quinn greeted them with his usual aplomb as he took Nash's hat, gloves, and cane.

"Thank you." Arabella hurried to the back of the house.

Nash shook his head as he watched her skirts flying down the corridor. Right now, he had more important matters on his mind. "Quinn, please have Cook send in coffee and a bite to eat. I'll be in my library most of the day."

"You have the Kendall ball this evening, my Lord." Andrews descended the stairs. "Please allow yourself time to dress." With those ominous words, Andrews marched past the two men and headed out the front door to continue supervising the unpacking of his lordship's trunks.

A sinking feeling landed in Nash's stomach. The Kendall affair would be the first time he and Arabella appeared in public since their hurried-up wedding. There was nothing to be done for it, though. They had to eventually face Society as a married couple. Hopefully, Arabella would present herself in a dignified manner. Aside from her indiscretion in rescuing the kitten at Blossom's farm, she'd done quite well in the country, but Town could be as dangerous as a battlefield, and just as bloody. Gossip, rumors, and innuendoes had never affected him before now, but he knew women, for all their softness and delicacy, were as vicious as the top commanders in the military. Except their weapons were their tongues, as sharp and dangerous as any saber.

If word of his countess's continued activities with injured animals reached the ears of some of the *ton*, it would be a social disaster for them both.

"Send for my solicitor, Mr. Manson." Nash nodded at Quinn and entered the library. He sat behind his large wooden desk and surveyed the room. Perhaps it was his marriage giving him a sense of settling down, perhaps not, but he found himself wishing to be back at Clarendon Manor.

It had been good seeing his tenants again and catching up on local gossip. Arabella seemed content there, as well. Of course, once they returned there after the Season, she would be sure to keep at him to build a larger kennel for her animals. Pushing all those matters aside, he removed his jacket and rolled up his sleeves. Pulling the large ledger book from the bottom drawer of his desk, he opened it, frowned at the numbers there, and set to work.

Nash impatiently brushed away Andrews's hands. "Enough. I am ready to go."

"My lord, this is your first appearance as a married gentleman. You do not want to disgrace Lady Clarendon."

Nash snorted. He would be lucky if Lady Clarendon didn't disgrace him by talking about her animals and the surgeries she'd performed. With his help, no less. Or perhaps a mouse would make its way into the ballroom, and she would find it necessary to crawl under furniture to retrieve it, her lovely bottom up in the air for all the men to admire.

He studied himself in the mirror. Black evening coat and breeches, with a silver and white waistcoat covering the stark white of his shirt. His intricately tied cravat made the freshly shaven skin on his face appear darker, swarthier.

He passed through his dressing room and gave a slight knock on Arabella's door. He stopped just inside the entrance, his eyes flickering from the top of her well-coiffed head to the dainty pink slippers peeking out from under her gown.

Arabella certainly looked the part of her ladyship, the Countess of Clarendon. Head held high, her eyes glimmered with what he could only surmise was determination. Was she ready to face the *ton*? She appeared to be.

"You look lovely, sweeting."

He pushed back his hair from his forehead and approached her. "Turn around, I have something for you."

She did as he bid. "These are the family jewels that

rightfully belong to the current countess." He fastened the latch and kissed the back of her neck, his warm breath causing gooseflesh to rise where his lips touched. "They look beautiful on you."

He held her shoulders and turned her so she faced him. He stood so close, he could smell her faint aroma of lavender and lemon. As he gazed down at her, her sparkling hazel eyes smiled more than her lips. Lips that urged him to kiss her. Warm, soft, moist. She opened her mouth at his slight nudge, and he entered, sweeping along, touching sensitive spots.

Arabella's tongue tangled with his, and he pulled her closer, wrapping his arm around her waist. His muscles tensed as he held her. Slowly, his hand came up, and he cupped her face, moving her head so he could take the kiss deeper. Her fingers wrapped around his arms, holding on.

Nash released her mouth and stepped back, his eyes eating her up. He ran his fingers down her cheek. "So sweet."

She closed her eyes at his gentle touch, and he reached into his pocket and took her gloved hand. After sliding a ring on her finger, he added a bracelet to her wrist, as well. "These are all part of the set, including these." He held up a pair of ruby and pearl earl bobs that matched the necklace, ring, and bracelet perfectly.

Taking the earrings from him with shaky hands, she slid them onto her earlobes. "It appears we are ready." She drew in a deep breath and slowly let it out, as if she were about to face her executioner. Perhaps that was how she felt.

He extended his arm, Arabella took it, and they left the room together, descending the steps to where Quinn held Nash's belongings. Once they were settled in the carriage, facing each other, Arabella began to fidget with the fasteners on her pelisse. "Since this is our first public appearance since the Ashbourne ball, I must admit to a small case of nerves."

"Understandable. However, we've nothing to be

concerned about. We are married now. You are my countess. You wear the family jewels. My mother approves of you. No doubt, after the first few minutes of gossiping, all attention will focus on the next scandal."

His jaw tightened. "However, please remember this is Polite Society, not the backwoods of my estate. No rushing to rescue an animal."

"That is the furthest thing from my mind right now. I do not like being the current scandal." She twisted her hands in her lap, staring at his shoes before turning her attention to the black sky outside the carriage window. "Do you intend for us to remain in London the entire Season?"

"I have my Parliamentary duties to see to. With the wedding and our trip to Suffolk, I am afraid I have missed a couple of important votes. I feel as though I need to be two people. One for Parliament, and one for Lord of the Manor. So, to answer your question, for the most part, yes."

Arabella nodded, lips tight, almost as though she knew that would be his answer. The ride continued in silence for a few minutes, the clopping of the horses' hooves bringing a rhythm that did not seem to soothe his wife.

"Arabella." Nash extended his hand to her. "Come here."

After a slight hesitation, she rose and moved next to him. He took her hands in his. "Even through our gloves I can feel how cold your hands are."

"Being the center of attention alarms me. Prior to now, I spent most of the Season courted by old men selected by my mother, fading into the background as much as I could otherwise."

"You are a beautiful woman, Arabella. It confuses me as to why your mother would push older men on you. Certainly, you would have had no problems attracting a young man."

"There were one or two that showed interest, but Mother felt an older man would 'take me in hand' and—I hate to say this, not live long, so I would be free to pursue my interests."

Nash's brows rose. "But you turned down those who offered. Had you no intention of ever marrying?"

"Oh, I knew, given my station, it was inevitable, unless I wished to be left afloat. I have no relatives who would have been willing to take on a spinster. A governess or companion might have solved that issue, but what of Mother?"

"You might have continued on at your country home. You mentioned the new earl was willing to allow you and your mother to stay."

"For how long? We have recently ascertained he is a single man with a duty to his new title. He would have needed to marry, and few new wives relish the idea of sharing their household with another woman. No, there was never a doubt I would one day wed, I merely wanted a couple of years to take my time."

He chuckled and squeezed her hand. "Instead you got three days."

"Yes. As did you." She gave him a soft smile. It seemed the conversation had relaxed her a bit.

The slow queue their carriage had been stuck in finally moved forward, and the vehicle rolled to a stop. A footman opened the door, and Nash stepped out, turning to assist Arabella. He placed her hand on his arm, and they made their way up the stairs to the Kendall townhouse. Arabella continued to take deep breaths, making him wonder if her stays were laced too tight. Lord, he hated those things.

Just as they arrived at the doorway to the ballroom, he leaned in and whispered into her ear, "Relax, sweetheart. 'Tis just another ball."

Arabella raised her head, and her lips lifted into a semblance of a smile. Once announced, they descended the stairs together. As expected, heads turned, whispers began behind decorated fans, and eyebrows rose. The muscles in

Nash's arm tightened, and he tugged her closer, covering the hand on his arm with his own.

The life they all led was ridiculous in so many ways. He and Arabella had been observed together in a dark library doing nothing more than conversing. Yet, she would have been a ruined woman who no gentleman would consider for his wife if he hadn't agreed to marry her. So foolish, but nonetheless the life they had been born into. And yet, now that they were married, they were still the object of gossip and idle chatter.

• • •

Arabella continued to grip Nash's arm as they made their way through the crowd, stopping to chat with various people. Most of them were Nash's friends, since he was a much more social person than she. Although a few ladies she had a passing acquaintance with did offer felicitations on her marriage.

What bothered her more were the number of young ladies and young matrons who stepped into their path to speak with Nash. For the most part, they ignored her, but more than a few seemed especially friendly with her husband. Not that she cared or was jealous, of course. It just made maneuvering around the room more awkward.

"Lord Clarendon!" Lady Walthrop, the young widow of the very aged Earl of Walthrop, waved to them as they moved away from a cluster of young ladies who'd spent most of the Season dropping their handkerchiefs at Nash's feet. Arabella tamped down her annoyance and put what she hoped looked like a smile on her face.

Lady Walthrop was beautiful. There was simply no other word. Golden-blond hair and the peaches-and-cream complexion so envied by the women of the *ton*. She'd been the Incomparable the year the Earl snatched her off the marriage mart, and he'd attempted for six months to get her with child before he dropped dead at his club. Rumor had it he'd found a footman in his wife's bed the night before. "Why, my Lord Clarendon. I hear you are married."

My Lord Clarendon?

Arabella gritted her teeth and smiled at the woman. At least she hoped it looked like a smile.

"Yes, allow me to present my countess." He turned to Arabella. "Lady Walthrop is an old friend."

Before Arabella could respond, the witch tapped Nash's arm with her fan. "Oh, please don't introduce me as an *old* friend." She tittered loud enough to draw attention, and Arabella wanted to stamp on her pretty satin slippers.

"You are right, my lady. Please accept my apologies. No one would consider you old." He smiled warmly at her, and Arabella wanted to gag. Instead she snorted, loud enough for Nash and the Incomparable to hear. But ignore.

The orchestra started a waltz, and Nash turned to her. "My dear, would you honor me with a dance?" He held out his hand.

Her stomach did a tap dance of glee as Lady Walthrop frowned. "Be sure to save a dance for me, my lord." The forward woman lowered her lashes like the sweet little debutante she no longer was.

Nash took her into his arms, and she relaxed for the first time since they'd entered the aballroom. "So, Lady Walthrop is an *old* friend?"

He studied her, the light from the many candles casting shadows on his strong features. He pulled her closer than what was considered proper and murmured in her ear. "To be perfectly frank, the woman scares me."

Arabella smiled. He didn't need to say any more.

"Trollop!"

The word had been whispered, but loud enough that both

Nash and Arabella heard it — as well as anyone within ten feet of Lady Grace, standing alongside the edge of the ballroom, fanning her face furiously. Her red cheeks and tightened lips marked her as the accuser.

Arabella stumbled, and Nash caught her. "Ignore her." He pulled her even closer and stared into her eyes. "Ignore her, sweeting," he repeated. "Hold your chin up. No one else here believes that."

"I am sure there are more than a few who do." Her attempt at humor fell flat.

"It doesn't count." He moved them so they were no longer within hearing, but Arabella saw the girl's mouth moving, her stance and demeanor telling.

Attempting to distract her, he said, "I found the trip to Suffolk less than satisfactory." He turned them to maneuver around another couple. "While you were charming my tenants, I had some serious conversations with the men. It is troubling that the elder Jones has gone to his daughter's home and his son is nowhere to be found, except to collect rents. I feel the need to make a return trip to Suffolk in a few weeks."

"Will we both be making the trip again?" What of her animals? She'd barely been able to check on their welfare before she'd had other duties to attend to, including a discussion with Mrs. McGregor. It amazed Arabella that so many issues had arisen in their short absence that had required her attention.

When Arabella had asked if the housekeeper had consulted her mother on the problems, she'd received a silent rebuke in the form of a sniff and a curt, "Lady Melrose is not my employer. Besides which, her ladyship has kept the staff busy with preparations to take up residence in Bath."

That had been news to Arabella. Perhaps it was for the best that Mother had taken Nash's suggestion that she might be happier in Bath. Having two women in the house could be difficult, and based on Mrs. McGregor's tone, she already viewed her mother's presence as problematic.

The final notes of the waltz came to an end. "Yes, we will both be traveling to Suffolk. I was under the impression you enjoyed your time there."

"I did. I was concerned for my animals."

His lips tightened, and he took her by the elbow. "I suggest we take a walk in the gardens to clear our heads."

Nash guided her toward the French doors leading to the patio. The air was sweet and cool and felt wonderful on her flushed face. They strolled the area, stopping to chat with couples also enjoying the evening air. So far, except for a few whispers when they'd entered, no one seemed to think there was anything untoward about the earl and his new countess.

Some of the guests had not received word of the marriage—hence they hadn't known about the potential scandal—but did seem confused seeing the two of them together. No doubt more than a few had been aware he'd been courting Lady Grace and had expected a betrothal announcement with her.

As they moved past Lord and Lady Mullens, Nash asked, "Would you care for some refreshment? You appear a bit flushed."

"Yes, I believe I would. I am rather parched."

After Nash left her for the refreshment table, Arabella wandered near the balustrade and gazed out upon the garden, with torches burning to light the pathway through the flowers. She realized her previous worries and anxiety had left her. Nash had been right. After the initial mumblings, smirks, and remarks cast in her direction at their entrance, she and her new husband had been relegated to the "no longer of interest" category. Most of the guests who had stopped them to chat had offered their felicitations and even extended invitations to events Arabella had never been invited to before.

"Lady Clarendon." It took Arabella a moment to realize someone was addressing her. She turned to Lady Lovell, who approached on the arm of her husband. The couple had been newly married a few months ago. Arabella and the then Lady Helen had come out the same year. "It is so nice to see you. Lovell and I have been in the country and just now returned to Town. And what is the first thing I hear but Lady Arabella is now Lady Clarendon!" Helen smiled at her. She had always been one of Arabella's favorite people.

"Yes. We are married a bare two weeks, in fact."

Lord Lowell looked around. "Where is the groom? Surely he has not abandoned you to the card room."

Arabella laughed at the condemnation in his tone. "Not at all. He is off to bring me a drink."

Helen regarded her. "No wedding trip?" Apparently, her friend had not heard the story of Arabella's disgrace. "No. But Clarendon and I have just returned from his country estate in Suffolk." At least that made it appear they'd had some type of wedding trip.

Lady Lovell's bright blue eyes lit up. "I intend to have my first dinner party in a few weeks, and I so wanted to include you. And your husband, of course." She lowered her voice as if groups of guests were listening to her party plans. "I will be very nervous, as you can imagine, so having you there would do much to calm my nerves."

"You will be fine, my dear." Lord Lovell patted his wife's arm. "It is not seemly to get yourself all worked up." Arabella smiled, thinking how lovely for Helen that her husband was so solicitous of her welfare. But then, theirs had been a love match.

"It seems some of the issues that arose while we visited the tenants have caused Clarendon some concern, and he plans a return trip sometime soon." Seeing the disappointment on her face, Arabella hurried on. "However, I will see if my husband can make our trip either before or after your dinner party. Just send the date around."

"My dear, I believe the next dance has started up." Lord Lowell addressed his bride then turned to Arabella. "I wish you and Clarendon well." He smiled and took his wife's hand, casting Helen a look that brought a smile to Arabella's face, and a bit of sadness to her heart.

She told herself she did not want that type of marriage. No feelings like that for her husband. Once that happened, all her freedom would be lost. She would begin following him around like one of her lost puppies, "yes, my lord" and "no, my lord" the only words on her lips.

As she watched the couple stroll away, Arabella's attention was caught by the sound of a female's voice uttering her name from the other side of the stone wall dividing the patio area from the garden.

"Oh, do not fool yourself, Diana. Lady Arabella and her mother set the entire thing up. I had personally witnessed Lady Arabella eying Lord Clarendon for some time. Apparently, she was unable to bring anyone up to scratch, so she and her devious mother decided to force the poor man into matrimony with her."

Arabella was unable to hear the response to Lady Grace's comments, since the person to whom she had spoken those untrue, vile words apparently faced the other direction. Lady Grace continued, "Not that it matters to me at all, you understand. I have had several offers and am contemplating one at this very moment. I have no regrets, nor had I intended to accept Lord Clarendon's offer, anyway."

Mumbling followed her words once again. Then, very clearly, Lady Grace's voice rang out. "Perhaps Lord Clarendon had been forced to marry her because she had granted him favors and found herself in a delicate condition? Not that I am saying that, you understand. But there have been rumors…"

Chapter Fifteen

Drink in hand, Nash approached Arabella just as Lady Grace's hateful words rang out in the darkened garden. Fortunately, no one remained on the patio to hear her vitriol, since the music had resumed. He took deep breaths to calm himself. The chit had gone beyond the bounds of decent behavior.

"Here you are, sweeting." He held out a glass of champagne. "I am afraid the ratafia was all gone. Not that I believe you prefer that over champagne," he joked.

Arabella accepted the glass with a shaky hand. His attempt to control his anger was less than successful. Her tightened lips fed the beast rising up to roar and strike out at the one who'd hurt someone under his care. It would certainly not be acceptable to tear around the corner and throttle the girl, but had she been a man that was precisely what he would have done.

Chewing on her bottom lip, Arabella avoided his eyes and sipped the drink. She placed the glass on a small table next to them as one lone tear slid down her cheek. She quickly swiped it from her cheek and looked at him, her chin raised.

Her face was pale in the moonlight, and she shuddered as if a sudden chill overtook her. His mind made up, he extended his arm. "Do you care for a walk, sweeting?"

Arabella glanced at the balustrade where Lady Grace and her cohorts stood. Straightening her shoulders, she studied him with narrowed eyes. From what he'd seen thus far, she was a strong woman who did not shy away from problems. Considering how well she'd accepted her mother's actions that had led to their forced marriage, plus all the animals she'd taken care of and nursed back to health—alone—his countess was no weakling.

But she was much too honest for the subterfuge of the *ton*. Cutting words and innuendoes were not her method of dealing with the world. Unfortunately, it was the means that many of the ladies of the *ton* employed. Curse their black hearts.

He tilted his head to one side and studied her, challenging her. "Yes?"

She stared back at him, a slight smile coming to her lips. Very kissable lips. "Yes, I believe I would enjoy a stroll. 'Tis truly a lovely evening, is it not?"

That's my girl.

Holding firmly onto his arm, they took the few steps into the garden. Lady Grace and two other young women stood near the wall, within plain sight of an older woman, a bit of distance from them, obviously one of their chaperones. Lady Grace's cheeks flushed at their appearance, but she raised her nose in the air as they approached.

"Good evening, ladies." Nash bowed slightly and turned his glare toward Lady Grace. "I am sorry, my lady, but I seem to have missed part of what you said about my wife just now. Care to repeat it?"

Lady Grace flushed a deeper red under the lights shining from the ballroom. "'Twas nothing, my lord." She curtsied.

Her two companions quickly followed suit, their faces also flushing.

His resilient wife stood by his side, her chin up, her eyes flashing. Nash drew her closer and covered the gloved hand on his arm with his. He had no doubt Arabella could handle herself, but as her husband and protector, it was his duty. "I do hope it was nothing, because I would be most upset if I heard untoward rumors bandied about regarding my countess." He looked directly at Lady Grace. "Surely you understand?"

When she did not answer, but continued to stare into the darkened garden, he added, "Lady Grace? Shall I assume you comprehend?"

Lady Grace glanced at him briefly and mumbled an acknowledgment. Stubborn little minx. And to think he'd almost married her. Her two companions looked decidedly uncomfortable. Nash turned his attention to them. "That goes for you, as well. The only whispers I expect to hear forthcoming about my wife will be complimentary ones." He paused, then added, "Am I correct in my assumption that there is nothing unclear about that?"

The two ladies nodded.

"Thank you, ladies. I wish you a pleasant evening." He moved away, and he and his wife continued their walk along the garden path, the smell of late spring flowers wafting in the air. Nash leaned in closer. "I believe it is over now."

When they were far enough away that she could not be heard by the young ladies, she said, "I am glad you did that."

His eyebrows rose. "Why would I not?"

Arabella shrugged. "You *were* about to make an offer for Lady Grace."

He smirked and patted her hand. "This is perhaps not the best time to remind me of that fact." Placing his arm around her shoulders, he pulled her close to his side when she continued to shiver. He turned them around, and they walked back toward the patio. Either nerves or the cool air was chilling her, and he did not want a reoccurrence of her illness. "Frankly, I was afraid if I did not defend you, that you would find a way to achieve satisfaction yourself." He grinned at her. "A critter of some sort or another in her carriage, perhaps?"

Once they reached the patio door, he opened it and escorted her through to the ballroom. She leaned up to whisper in his ear. "You read my mind, my lord."

His laughter had heads turning in their direction.

• • •

The following week, at the end of a long day of dealing with household matters, Arabella picked up her skirts and hurried up the stairs to the second floor of the townhouse. She reached the corridor and walking briskly, her head down as she thought of the ball that evening, ran directly into Nash as he left his bedchamber. He grabbed her shoulders. "Slow down, sweeting, where are you off to?"

Startled from the collision, she reared back. "Oh. My apologies. I am going to check on my animals."

"You do remember the Kensington ball this evening?"

She bristled. He had been watching over her shoulder all week. Just yesterday, when he'd heard Quinn announce that Lady Matilda and her daughter, Miss Petunia, had called, Nash had dragged her into her bedchamber and instructed her on how to conduct herself.

Rounding on him, she'd said, "My lord, although you have very little faith in my ability to conduct myself, please know that I have not lived under a rock these past years. Mother and I oftentimes made and received afternoon calls."

Now he wanted to make sure she would not forget an event she'd been reminded of extensively. "I am unlikely to forget, since you've repeated the message several times,

Sophia has already laid out my gown, and Andrews took it upon himself to order me a bath. Honestly, it is as though no one thinks I have a brain in my head."

"I am trying to secure our place in Society. It is important to me, as it should be to you, as well."

"Why? No one cares if I attend or not. Lady Grace will be looking for any opportunity to malign me, your *old* friend, Lady Walthrop will be just breathless with anticipation at your arrival, and I will undoubtedly do something to call attention to myself."

"If you behave yourself as a countess should, you will not call attention to yourself."

Oh, his arrogance was unequaled. With a curt nod, she swept past him then stopped at the doorway to the room where her recovering animals were. "Please instruct Cook to send a tray to my room. I will be too busy preparing for the ball to dine with you."

By the time she closed the door, she was breathing heavily and mad enough to scream. But then, a countess never screamed. Or called attention to herself. Or handled animals.

It seemed ever since the Kendall ball, Nash had found one thing or another to criticize her for that had left her wanting. The closeness she'd felt after he defended her had been slowly chiseled away over time. Perhaps he felt Lady Grace's criticism of her was justified, after all.

She took a deep breath to calm herself and focused on her furry friends. "Good evening, everyone." Her spirits rose as she checked each animal under her care and fussed with the bandage on the small pug she'd found a few days before. The poor thing had a large splinter in its paw that she'd carefully removed before applying a salve and bandage.

She moved to the next box and sucked in a deep breath. The poor little bird she'd rescued from a cat's mouth had died. She hated when her efforts did not work. There would be no time for a quick burial, since she had to prepare for the ball. Truthfully, she'd rather bury the bird.

With a sigh, she left the room. Duty called.

"My lady, you look stunning!" Sophia stood back and admired the work she'd done on Arabella. Her gown of crimson red silk with a white net embroidered overlay, cap sleeves off the shoulders, and a low-cut bodice, highlighted the alabaster white of her creamy skin and the slight flush to her cheeks.

Her long white satin gloves left only a few inches of skin on her arm exposed. Sophia had brushed her hair into a fine gloss and pulled the curls up to the crown of her head to cascade down her back. A curl had been left on each side to dangle by her ears.

Arabella viewed herself in the mirror and was pleased. Her ensemble gave her the confidence she needed to face Society once again. "Sophia please fetch the ruby necklace and matching pieces. They will go well with this gown."

A tap on the door between their bedchambers drew her eyes to where Nash appeared. His eyes raked her seductively, the look tightening her nipples and sending a message to her lower parts. Slowly she raised her chin, thrilled at the effect she'd had on him. "I am almost ready."

In a few lengthy strides, he was across the room and standing in front of her, his hand out to Sophia. "I'll finish up, Sophia. You may leave now." His eyes never left hers, and the depth of his voice sent chills washing over her. To the point where she shivered.

Sophia deposited the jewelry into his outstretched hand and scurried away, a smirk on her face.

Apparently aware of tension between then, Nash gave Arabella a slow grin and did a quick circular movement with his finger, indicating she should turn. She had full view of them both in the mirror. Nash's swarthy skin above his starched cravat, the blond curls teasing his forehead, and his darkened blue eyes, staring at her intently.

He set the pieces on the dressing table and placed his hands on her shoulders. Brushing aside her curls, his head descended, the warm moistness of his breath teasing the hair at her nape. She closed her eyes as his lips touched her skin. She jolted at the contact and let out a soft moan.

Her head fell to one side as he kissed, nipped, and licked the delicate skin. A slow, dull ache began between her legs, and her knees felt about to give in. Sensing her need, he wrapped one strong arm around her waist to hold her up, pressing her against his hard body. With his other hand, he turned her head, and his mouth covered hers hungrily.

His mouth slid to her jaw, her neck, the sensitive skin behind her ear. "What do you say we skip this ball and find other, more pleasing ways to occupy our time?"

For once, Arabella did want to attend a ball. She felt confident and loved the way she looked. Tonight, she would show the *ton* that she truly *was* a countess.

Nash tucked his hand into her bodice and fingered her nipple. Oh, the man was convincing. She purred as he kissed her neck again and did wonderful things with his naughty finger. Just as she was ready to rid herself of her lovely gown, Nash pulled back and sighed. "I am sorry, sweetheart, but this is one ball we do need to attend."

She stared up at him, still lost in the feelings he'd evoked. "Why?"

He reached for the necklace on the dressing table. "Two of the lords I need to help push through my bill in Parliament will be there. It is almost impossible to get these men together, and this might be my only chance."

Her head spinning, she nodded and allowed him to fasten

the necklace. She took the rest of the pieces from him and quickly added them to her arm, finger, and ears. By the time she finished, she'd almost recovered from his passionate assault. Taking a deep breath to release any remnants from their love play, she smiled and accepted his arm.

. . .

It had taken all of Nash's control to pull back from Arabella and to think of his duty. If his bill, which was important to the members of the army, was not passed this session, the soldiers would face another year of ill-equipped quarters and insufficient pay. Lords Dressen and Tamlin were close to agreeing and only needed one more push. Especially, if they knew that both of them supported the bill.

However, one glance at Arabella and he had wanted nothing more than to strip that beautiful gown off her and spend hours in bed, kissing every inch of her nude body. At times, it was difficult to remember one's duty and carry through. He comforted his raging erection with the thought that once they returned home, he would see to another sort of duty to his title.

He could not stop staring at her on the way to the Kensington ball. The soft light from the lantern on the inside of the carriage highlighted the golden streaks in her hair. Her lips were still plump from his kiss, and her perfectly arranged hair had been mussed a bit. When had she grown so seductive? He'd desired her almost from the first, but this was something different.

Was it the gown, or had she changed? Or perhaps she hadn't changed at all, but he'd never noticed her strong sexual appeal. He shifted in his seat, slightly annoyed that other men would have the opportunity to ogle her.

Their arrival at this ball was markedly different than

the last one. Arabella held her head high, confidence in her every movement. His muscles tightened at the stares she was receiving from the men in the room. Had they no one else to gape at? He took her small hand resting on his arm in his and wrapped his arm around her waist. A definite possessive move that was very unlike him. She looked at him, a slight smile that had heat rising to his face. Bloody hell, he was acting like a lovestruck half-wit, the type of man he'd always pitied.

He frowned when Lord Applegate, trailed by two other fools, moved toward them, Applegate's eyes practically falling out of his muddled head. "My lady." He bowed and took her extended hand. "You are looking spectacularly enchanting this evening."

Nash snorted as Arabella did a slight dip and blushed prettily. "Thank you, my lord."

Mr. Marshall, a known libertine and third son of the Earl of Lancaster, was next to bow and stare at Arabella's breasts. Nash ran his finger around the inside of his cravat. He would need to find the two lords he must speak with and whisk Arabella home. She was not used to this attention, and she was probably very uncomfortable.

"May I request to be added to your dance card, my lady?" Applegate broke into a foolish grin that had Nash itching to punch it off his ridiculous face. Of course, it would be good manners for Arabella to accept, but since he knew her so well, he would excuse this lapse of good behavior when she refused him.

"Yes, my lord. I would be delighted to add you to my dance card." She lowered her lashes and held out the small card dangling from her wrist.

Good lord, the woman was flirting! He looked back and forth between Applegate and Arabella, his mouth agape. Before he had recovered his senses, Marshall, and the other man with their group, Lord Boyle, had written their names on her dance card as well. Nash grabbed a glass of champagne from a passing footman and gulped it down as he watched his wife—who liked to sew up bloody animals—banter with three of the most notorious members of the *ton*.

The orchestra started up a waltz, and setting the glass in his hand on a nearby table, Nash took Arabella's hand. "My dear. I believe this is my dance."

She tilted her head, her eyes sparkling. "Did you write your name on my dance card?"

He growled and tugged her away from her admirers, holding her hand tightly as he led her to the dance floor. He spun her around into his arms, gripping her waist, his face close to hers. "I do not need to write my name on your dance card."

Arabella shrugged. "I was merely asking, my lord." The grin on her face riled him even more.

The dance number began, and they moved with the music. "You are very popular tonight, my dear." Lord, he hated how his voice sounded. He was leaving himself open for her scorn. The last thing he wanted was for her to think he was jealous. Which he was not, of course, but there was no reason to make her believe that.

"Do you think so?" She seemed actually pleased.

"I thought you did not enjoy the attentions of the *ton*." Could she hear the desperation in his voice? He needed to pull himself together before she burst out laughing. Taking a deep breath, he turned them to avoid another couple.

"I find I do not mind it so much this evening. Perhaps I have been misjudging people."

She had not been misjudging people, she had merely been dressed as the wallflower she'd thought herself to be. Only good enough for old men. He pulled her closer, their thighs touching as they moved in a circle.

"Nash, I don't think this is respectable." She tried to ease back. He was having none of it. She belonged to him, and everyone here would know it.

He leaned in, whispering in her ear. "When we get home, I will show you how very *unrespectable* I can be."

Her breath hitched. "I don't think that's a word."

"No matter. What I have in mind does not require words." He spun her around, noting how weak her legs seemed as she clung to him. "Trust me."

Chapter Sixteen

Arabella was certain Sophia had laced her stays too tight. Ever since Nash had entered her bedroom earlier, she'd had trouble breathing. Now with the look on his face, and his comments, she was sure she'd faint dead away.

His muscled arm was tight against her waist, his hand splayed across her lower back. Muscular thighs encased in satin breeches—which were now touching her legs in a most inappropriate manner—along with his black waistcoat and tailcoat gave him a very rakish look.

Their entrance down the stairs to the ballroom had been much friendlier this time. She couldn't help but think it had a great deal to do with her husband. Every woman they passed had eyed him as if he were the next course in their dinner. Were she not so annoyed at their forwardness, she might have giggled at the two young ladies who dropped their handkerchiefs in his path.

Thankfully, he had missed it. He seemed too taken up with the few gentlemen who had requested dances from her. She thought it was very nice of them, since she would no doubt have a mostly empty dance card.

The music came to an end. Nash seemed reluctant to let her go. She viewed him with curiosity as she attempted to move out of his arms. "Nash? I believe I would like a glass of lemonade before my next dance."

"Certainly, my dear." Keeping his hand on her lower back, he walked her back to the crowd at the edge of the dance floor. He maneuvered her around several gentlemen who seemed to want to speak to them and right to a group of elderly matrons, who immediately invited her into their conversation about their various ailments.

Confused at his behavior since they'd arrived, she watched him make his way back to the refreshment table. Lady Humphries tapped her on the arm with her fan. "No point in watching him, dear, men will do what they want. You best remember that." She tapped her cane on the floor to emphasize her point.

"I beg your pardon?" What did the woman mean?

"I know you are recently married, but you might as well learn the way of it. Your mother should have told you. But if she hasn't, then I will." She leaned in close, the smell of her breath bringing tears to Arabella's eyes. "Men have mistresses."

Arabella continued to stare at her. "Mistresses?"

"Yes. You might as well accept it, gel. Get what you can from him in the way of jewels, gowns, and trips. Give him an heir and a spare and then go your own way, too." She winked.

Arabella drew back, running her tongue over her lips. "If you will excuse me, my lady."

Despite wanting to rush from the room to the patio to get fresh air, her way was blocked by one man after another, requesting dances. As soon as she reached out to open the door, a large hand covered hers. "Where are you off to? I thought you were thirsty."

She turned and gave Nash a bright smile. "I felt the need for some air. 'Tis quite crowded in here."

Nash took her hand, intertwining their fingers, and escorted her out the door, still holding two glasses of champagne in his other hand. He led her to an empty table and placed the drinks down. "You do look a bit flushed." He joined her and slid a glass in front of her.

Should she come right out and ask him?

I am just curious, my lord. How is your mistress?

Trying not to be obvious, she studied him under lowered lashes. He certainly was handsome enough. Even though she'd known him for a while through Eugenia, she'd never taken particular notice of his looks. It was well known among the Quality that the Earl of Clarendon was an excellent catch. Even after he had turned his attention to Lady Grace, the other young ladies had continued to do whatever it was they could, within the bounds of propriety, to gain his notice.

After the display she'd seen this evening, with women, young and old, following him with their eyes, it appeared he was still quite popular with the ladies. Something ugly inside of her twisted and called out to let the world know Lord Clarendon was taken. He was hers. Maybe not by choice, but nevertheless, still hers.

"What? You're looking at me like you want to snap my head off." Nash took the last sip of his drink.

She would never let him know she was jealous. Of course, she wasn't jealous, only that she did not want to be made a fool of by having women draped all over her husband in public. "It seemed to take quite a long time for you to bring my drink."

His eyes grew wide. "A long time?" He leaned in and lowered his voice. "Not as long as it took you to make your way through the ballroom what with stopping every man in your path so he could write his name on your dance card."

Arabella gritted her teeth. "They were stopping *me*. I was

anxious to wade through the crowd and inhale some fresh air."

Nash opened his mouth to speak when a voice interrupted them. "Oh, here you are my lady. 'Tis time for our dance." Lord Applegate walked toward them, his hand extended.

"Her foot hurts," Nash snapped.

Arabella's jaw dropped. "No, it doesn't!" She stood and took Lord Applegate's hand. Whatever was the matter with him? If she didn't know better, she would think he was jealous of the attention she was getting. Foolish thought, that.

He stood and walked with them to the ballroom doors. "I am glad to see you are feeling better, my dear. If you wish to return home, I will be happy to escort you."

She drew herself up and cast him her stoniest glare. "No, thank you. I am fine. Please excuse us." Wanting to slap the silly grin off Lord Applegate's face, she glared in his direction, too, and then placed her hand on his arm.

Not as muscular as Nash's.

They joined the line of dancers just as the music started up.

• • •

Nash leaned against the wall, arms crossed, and watched Arabella and Applegate as they joined the dance. He felt like a fool and wanted more than anything to take back his stupid remark about her foot. Applegate was still grinning.

The idiot.

He smelled her scent before he saw her. Overpowering roses and some other mysterious fragrance. With a slight groan, he turned to face Lady Walthrop. If the woman took in a deep breath, her charms would tumble out of her bodice. She leaned against him, her fan tapping his chest. "I have been looking for you, my lord."

"Indeed?"

She raised her slender arm and waved her hand back and forth so the card tied there swung in front of his face. "I do not see your name on my dance card." She grinned. "A mistake, I am sure."

He bowed. "Of course. It is just that I have not seen you yet this evening."

She pouted, something that had probably looked adorable when she was the darling of the *ton*, but now appeared false and contrived. "I will not accept that, my lord. You looked directly at me when you first arrived."

When he'd been watching all the men who were ogling his wife.

"Then it is definitely time to have my vision checked, my lady." He took her card and scribbled his name on an empty spot.

She glanced at the card. "Oh, how wonderful. You have the supper waltz." Before he could say anything, she patted his cheek and said, "Now I must be off. Mr. Garvey has the next dance." She swept away, leaving behind her scent and his stomach in knots.

Bloody hell. How would he explain to Arabella that Lady Walthrop had claimed the supper dance? That also meant his wife would be free to waltz with someone else and then take supper with him. That yet-unknown man would be free to gaze at her rounded breasts each time she took a breath.

Said unknown libertine was a dead man.

Two young ladies strolled up to him with Lord Abbott. The man introduced them as his sister, Lady Miranda, and her friend, Miss Ellis. Both ladies were young, most likely fresh out of the schoolroom. Exactly the type of girl he'd been avoiding most of his adult life until he had decided to take a bride and focused on Lady Grace. But now, it mattered not, since he was married.

Being the proper gentleman, he wrote his name on their dance cards and waited for his wife to finish her dance with Applegate. Once they joined their little circle, Nash spotted Lord Dressen across the room, speaking with another member of the House of Lords. Finding the perfect opportunity to convince the man to support his bill, he excused himself from the group and headed in the man's direction.

No sooner had they begun to talk than the next dance started. He explained the necessity of passing the bill all the while watching Arabella dance a lively country dance with Marshall. Did she have to bounce up and down so much? Her breasts were having a fine time with all that jiggling, and Marshall was having as good of a time studying them. Once he blackened the man's eyes it would be some time before he could leer at another woman.

"I say, Clarendon, you seem a bit distracted." Dressen regarded him through his quizzing glass.

"My apologies." He pulled his attention away from Arabella and tried his best to concentrate on what the man was rambling on about. He'd already gotten his assurance he would vote in favor of the bill. Now he was regaling Nash with stories about his hounds.

More animals. He was truly cursed.

He finally disentangled himself from Dressen and hailed Lord Tamlin. Twice, his conversation with him was interrupted by promised dances to young ladies. In the meantime, he'd lost track of Arabella. He'd catch her laughing and dancing with some gentleman, and then she'd be gone again.

The orchestra had been silent for some time when Nash finally realized the music had stopped. The noise from all the various conversations was beginning to give him a headache. He said his farewell to Tamlin and began to search for Arabella. He turned suddenly when there was a light tap on his shoulder.

"The orchestra is returning. It is time for the supper waltz." Arabella beamed at him, causing him to break into a smile. She was flushed from all the dancing, her hair was not quite as set as it had been when they'd arrived, and she looked absolutely beautiful.

"It appears you have been having a good time." He took her hand in his and kissed the back of her wrist, wishing it was bare skin and not her glove.

"Yes. But I believe I am ready for some supper, and then maybe a return home?" Her voice was low and sultry, and she tilted her head in a coquettish manner.

His blood boiled, and his cock shouted "hurrah." Precisely what he had in mind. The first notes of the waltz began just as Lady Walthrop tapped him on the arm. He'd completely forgotten about her and now wished he had left earlier. Arabella viewed her with raised eyebrows.

"I believe you indicated your desire to have me for the supper waltz, my lord?" She held up the dance card dangling from her wrist, her eyes telling him she worded her statement as she had on purpose.

He turned his head to where Arabella stood next to him. He could probably cook his dinner over the steam coming from her ears. He stepped closer to Lady Walthrop, afraid for her well-being. His wife took in an exceptionally deep breath and raised her chin. "I will see you after supper, my lord." With that pronouncement, she turned on her heel and moved away from him.

Lady Walthrop gave him a siren's smile. "The music is starting."

He took her hand in his and led her to the dance floor. He kept a decent amount of space between them, even though his dance partner seemed to have other ideas.

Bloody, bloody hell.

• • •

I will not cry. I will not cry. I will not cry. The words pounded in Arabella's head as she pushed her way through the throng of dancers and headed for the ladies' retiring room. She kept a smile plastered on her face.

How dare the man arrange to have the supper waltz and meal with that trollop? She was hanging all over him, patting him on the chest, and staring up into his eyes. Eyes she wanted to scratch out.

Is Lady Walthrop his mistress?

The thought almost brought her to her knees. She'd best take a deep breath and compose herself. She was beginning to think like a jealous wife. She was not a jealous wife. If he wanted to take mistresses, it would not be her concern.

Then why did the thought of Nash doing all the wonderful things he did to her to another woman cause her stomach to cramp? Too confused and hurt to overly examine her feelings, she almost made it out of the ballroom when Lord Munro stepped in front of her. "Lady Clarendon! Certainly, surely you are not without a partner?"

"It seems I am, my lord." Well, apparently, her brain and mouth still functioned.

"Then I must rectify that situation immediately." He extended his arm, a broad smile on his face. She looked up at the man towering over her. Not classically handsome, nevertheless his strong features drew the attention of many of the young ladies. He was slender, yet still filled out his jacket well. His dark hair was done in one of those fancy styles she did not particularly like, but overall, his appearance was quite pleasing.

Why should she sit out the dance and supper in the ladies' retiring room? Hadn't she done enough of that before she married, avoiding the old men her mother pushed on her?

She reached out and placed her hand on his arm. "I will be happy to accompany you, my lord."

He swept her into his arms, and they joined the couples on the floor. He was an excellent dancer and kept up a lively conversation.

But he wasn't Nash.

Lord Munro turned her, and she got a glimpse of Nash and Lady Walthrop. She was happy to see Nash looking around, his lips tightening when his eyes rested on her. She took the opportunity to gaze up at Lord Munro and laughed as if he'd said something funny.

They spent the rest of the dance glaring at each other every time they came into view. The supper was no better. Lord Munro offered to have them sit with Nash and Lady Walthrop. She declined, since she wasn't completely sure she would not dump her supper plate in the woman's lap.

He seemed uncomfortable with the situation, and even though he tried, very hard, to entertain her, she only gave Lord Munro scant attention. No sooner had she put down her fork than Nash was by her side. "I believe you indicated a desire to return home once supper was finished?"

Arabella looked around, but Lady Walthrop was nowhere to be seen. "Yes. I am feeling a bit weary." She smiled at Lord Munro. "If you will excuse me, my lord." She stood and took Nash's arm, and they strolled around the room on the way to the exit. They were stopped a few times and exchanged pleasantries.

The entire time Arabella was stiff as a board, and the muscles in Nash's arm were tight under her hand. Neither looked at the other, and their comments to other guests were no more than inane platitudes.

Eventually they found themselves in the entrance hall, waiting for their carriage. Nash helped her on with her pelisse and handed her reticule to her. They were the only guests waiting for a carriage, since the orchestra had started up again.

Arabella had her arms wrapped around her body, trying to protect herself from the feelings racing through her. She had never wanted any of this. Why did she care if he preferred someone else? They had no claim on each other. Husbands and wives were not supposed to live in each other's pockets anyway. From what she'd seen, many of them did not even attend the same affairs.

She had a nice life. Mother was taken care of, she had her animals, a lovely home, and one day there would probably be a child or two.

An heir and a spare, then you go you can go your own way, too.

There was no fighting it. For better or worse, this was their world.

Nash took her arm and helped her down the stairs. Once she was in the carriage, he held the door open and called up to the driver. "Keep driving until I tap on the ceiling."

Whatever did that mean? If he thought to complain to her again about the men she'd danced with, he would find she had quite a bit to say to him, as well.

Nash settled in across from her. They remained silent until the carriage was well on its way from Kensington's townhouse. "Did you have a nice time this evening?" The tightness in his voice sparked something fierce in her.

"Oh my, yes. I had a wonderful time. I enjoyed so many dances with so many handsome and attentive men. It was truly delightful."

"Don't…" He growled. His eyes narrowed, and his finger tapped a cadence on his thigh.

She raised her brows at him. "Don't?"

"Do not say anything else." He rolled his neck as if to relieve tension.

"I am sorry, my lord. I was under the impression you

asked me a question."

Before the words were completely out of her mouth, Nash reached across the small space and wrapping his hands around her arms, pulled her over to his side. She landed on his lap. "What—"

He placed both of his hands on her head and took her mouth with a savage intensity.

Chapter Seventeen

Still gripping her head, Nash pushed her back, staring into her eyes, seeking consent. She watched him back, not with fear or anger, but with a passionate fire he'd never seen before, but certainly recognized.

With a growl worthy of a wild animal claiming its mate, he regained her lips, crushing her body to his. He was not looking for softness or gentleness tonight. What he needed from her right now was brutal, passionate surrender. To show her to whom she belonged.

He was crazy. That was the only explanation. He had lost his mind. This woman had turned him into an addlebrained fool whose future, no doubt, rested in Bedlam. Watching one man after another stare at her beauty, receive her smile, and ogle the creamy expanse of skin above her neckline had pushed him over the brink of the sanity he normally possessed.

Mine. Only mine.

Releasing her lips, he kissed her cheek, her closed eyelids, her jaw, her neck. Yes, her neck! He sucked on the skin there and nipped the soft flesh. She would have a bruise in the morning, and he cared not. He needed to mark her as his for all the world to see.

Grabbing the flaps of her pelisse, he jerked it apart, the fasteners flying in every direction. With a soft moan, her head fell back, and he yanked the garment off her shoulders, down her arms, and tossed it on the floor. He burrowed his fingers in her hair and sucked her earlobe. "I need you tonight."

"Yes." Her whispered consent spurred him on, adding to the craziness.

He spoke against her lips. "Right here. Right now."

"Yes, yes." She turned in his lap, her legs straddling him, her gown up around her thighs. She took his face in her hands and sucked his lower lip, then swept her tongue into his mouth. His hands slid under her gown, up her legs until he cupped her soft, plush bottom.

His entire world had narrowed to this small space where breathing was rapid and loud, clothing was in the way, and the scent of their passion filled the air. Arabella pulled at his cravat, almost strangling him until he took over and untied it, pulling it off and dropping it.

He kneaded her buttocks, pulling her closer to his cock, straining to get out of his breeches and slip into her warmth. Her lips, plump and moist, teased him, dared him, challenged his power. Power to own her, mark her, make her completely his. There was no tenderness in their need for each other tonight.

Nash fisted the edge of her gown and pulled it down, the sound of a tear competing with their raspy breaths. He groaned at the sight of two perfect, fleshy breasts with dark pouting nipples.

"Nash, you tore my gown." She spoke against his lips.

"I hate this gown."

"You said you loved it."

"I lied."

His mouth found other, more important uses than conversation. He sucked her breast into his mouth, then used his teeth to graze over the nipple. Arabella jerked and frantically shoved his tailcoat off his shoulders. Next went the waistcoat, and finally, he released her breast to pull his shirt over his head and added it to the pile of clothing on the floor.

Arabella rose up on her knees and rubbed her breasts against his chest and once more grabbed his head, running her fingers through his hair, tugging and pulling as she dragged him to her mouth for another searing kiss. He had no sense of time and place. He felt as though he had been born here and never wanted to leave.

She released him, and with a devilish smile moved her hands to his falls. Staring at him intently, she slowly opened each button, pausing to lick her lips between each one, until he thought he would lose his mind.

She reached her hand in and took his cock into her fist, running her fingers up and down his length. Before he realized what she was about, she climbed off his lap, knelt on the floor of the carriage between his legs, and wrapping her arms around his waist, took him into her mouth. He nearly jumped off the seat. She looked up at him, laughter in her eyes.

There was no doubt. She would kill him before the night was over.

He took about as much of that as he could before he grabbed her under her arms and hauled her back onto his lap. He fumbled with the fastenings at the back of her gown, and eventually it went the same way the pelisse did. Fastenings pinging against the walls of the carriage.

Within minutes he had her completely nude except for her jewelry, long white satin gloves, and silky white stockings. Just that slight bit of clothing tantalized him like nothing else. If he didn't have her now, he would explode. His hips rose, and he slid his breeches off then positioned her over his straining erection and eased her down over his length. He gritted his teeth and closed his eyes at the sensations running through him.

He took a breast into his mouth and suckled hard. She moaned and wiggled around.

"Darling, you are killing me." He barely got the words out with his breathing so ragged that he felt as if he'd just gone through five rounds at Gentleman Jackson's.

Gripping her hips, he moved her up and down until she caught the rhythm. Then rising up onto her knees, she took over, holding his shoulders as she moved. Her motion was perfect, her head thrown back, the beady points of her nipples teasing him as she shifted, her breasts swaying with the flow of her body.

"Nash, it's coming, I can feel it," she gasped, her voice raspy, her breathing erratic. Her hair had come undone, the riot of brown and golden curls falling over her shoulders, down her back.

He felt all her muscles tense as she tried to reach her climax. Helping her along, Nash reached between them and took the stiff piece of throbbing flesh and rubbed his thumb over the slick skin.

"Yes, yes. That's it." Her movements grew more frantic, and he gritted his teeth struggling to hold on until she reached her release. Just as he believed he could not wait a moment longer, she threw her head back and a low, keening sound came from her throat.

Nash let go and poured himself into her, pumping until every drop of fluid left his body.

• • •

Arabella was plastered against Nash's body, gulping air, trying to return her heart to a normal beat. It didn't sound as though he was doing any better, either, as he rested his chin on her shoulder. His sweat-dampened hair rested on her cheek.

She could not understand how they could be so mad at each other one minute and then tear each other's clothes off in a frenzy.

But it had felt good.

She had behaved the wanton. Now that she was coming back to her senses, she squirmed a bit with the memory. For goodness' sake, they were in a moving carriage! Had the driver heard them?

Nash moved his hand up and slowly massaged her head. "Do not fret, sweetheart."

She shifted and looked over at him. He gazed at her, a slight crooked smile on his lips. His swollen lips. Had she done that?

"You are beginning to experience some sort of remorse or guilt."

"How do you know that?" Lord, her voice still sounded raspy. Had she screamed her release?

"Your body stiffened. You began to shift around, and now as I study you, a lovely red flush is climbing up your body."

She pushed back, resting her hands on his sweat-slicked shoulders. "We are in our carriage."

"I know." He grinned.

The wicked man.

"The driver probably knows what we did."

He shook his head and pushed back the hair from her face. "No. Believe me, sweetheart, with the horses' hooves clopping along, and the wagon wheels creaking, he heard nothing."

"I'm getting chilly."

"Yes, I imagine you are." He reached to the floor and pulled up a mass of entangled garments. "We'll need to get this all sorted out. We don't want you entering the house in my cravat, and me in your gown."

She burst out laughing at the image, needing the release of tension.

Nash held up her stays. "This I would like to burn." He ran his hands over her breasts. "I like you much better this way."

"No respectable woman goes without her stays."

He grinned. "Who says I want a respectable woman?"

"Pardon me? Is not that what you have been chastising me about since we met?" She grabbed his cravat and wrapped it around his neck, as if to strangle him.

He covered her hand with his. "Yes, I want a respectable countess in my home, at social affairs, and everywhere in public. On the other hand, I want a wanton trollop in my bed." He winked.

Lord, if her face grew any hotter she would burst into flames. Taking a deep breath to bring up the subject troubling her, she twisted a strand of her hair and asked, "Nash, is Lady Walthrop your mistress?"

Nash reared back and sucked in a huge breath of air, then began to cough until Arabella had to pound him on the back. "Whatever made you ask that?"

Arabella drew circles on his chest. "Lady Humphries told me tonight that all men keep mistresses. Since you saved the supper waltz for Lady Walthrop, I wondered…"

He groaned and dropped his chin onto his chest. After a few moments, he looked up, staring in her eyes. "Hear this, Wife." He ran his fingers through his hair. "I can't believe I'm even speaking with you about this."

Her muscles tensed while she waited for his answer, and she pulled back. He wrapped his hands around her upper back and drew her forward until they were practically nose-to-nose. "When I was a single man, I maintained a mistress, as most men do. However, once we announced our betrothal, I dismissed her. I have no intention of breaking my marriage vows.

"As to your other supposition, Lady Walthrop spends a great deal of time inviting men into her bed. Even if I were in the market for a liaison, I can assure you, it would never be her. The reason we had the supper waltz was because when she handed me her card and insisted I fill it out, I wrote my name, not looking at it. I just wanted to be rid of her."

Arabella felt as though a huge boulder had been lifted from her shoulders. Not because she was jealous, she assured herself. She did not love Nash, had no intention of ever doing so, but she would have found it hard to face Society if her husband's mistress was present at these events.

"I would like to add one thing." Nash cupped her chin and kissed her softly. "I expect the same loyalty from you. If I know Lady Humphries as well as I think I do, I am sure she advised you to produce an heir and a spare and then take your own lover."

She nodded.

He shook his head. "No. That will never happen."

He tapped her on the nose. "Now I suggest we get dressed as best we can and go home. I find I am up for a repeat of tonight's activities. Only this time I would prefer a nice, soft bed."

It was encouraging that they agreed on some things, Arabella thought, as she riffled through the pile of discarded clothing. She needed to appear somewhat dignified when they walked into the house.

Chapter Eighteen

Three weeks later, Nash sat behind his desk in the library, gazing out the window at the cloudy day. The prior evening, the second meeting for the investors in the Indian cloth venture had gone well. The man who'd conducted the meeting had laid out a plan that involved a certain amount of risk, but in the end, could reap a tidy reward for those willing to take the chance.

Nash was willing.

He'd agreed to invest a good portion of Arabella's dowry, leaving the rest for needed repairs and new equipment to improve production on his tenants' farms. Which led him to thoughts of the audience his man of business had requested this morning. He'd set Mr. Bowers on a quest to gather as much information as he could about Mr. Jones and his son, who had been collecting the rents and only turning over part of it.

Although irritated at being duped, he at least had a sense of his financial situation not being as dire as he'd thought. Once he placed a trustworthy man in the steward's position, things should begin to turn around.

"My lord, Mr. Bowers has requested an audience." Quinn stepped aside as his man of business entered the room.

"Thank you, Quinn. Please have Cook send in coffee and some pastries."

Quinn bowed and quit the room. Nash waved to the chair in front of him. "Have a seat. I'm anxious to hear your report."

Bowers removed his spectacles and rubbed the lenses with a handkerchief. Once they were sufficiently polished and adjusted to his satisfaction on his face, he picked up his papers and studied them. Nash held in a smile at the way Bowers prepared himself for meetings.

The man cleared his throat three times, then began. "My lord, it appears you were correct, and Mr. Jones, the younger, has been assuming his father's duties as steward for the past many months. It was during this time that he raised the tenants' rents." He stopped and looked up at Nash. "Without your permission. And kept the extra money for himself. He also received more money for the crops and livestock than he entered in his books."

Bowers drew out his handkerchief and mopped his face. Taking a deep breath, he continued. "Notations made for repairs on buildings, fences, and roads were all false. Most repairs were made for a good deal less than reported, and some repairs were never done at all, although he took money for them.

"I had someone make an inspection of all the farms and outlying areas encompassing your estate, and I am sorry to report there are repairs that need to be done immediately, as well as some improvements that would help the farmers, and in turn, yourself, that should have been done already."

His man continued on, reading from his notes, and although Nash's mind began to drift from his actual words, what came across quite clearly was the Clarendon estate had been robbed blind.

Once Bowers finished, Nash rose and walked to the window and stared out at the gardens. For generations, men had lost all their money as well as un-entailed holdings due to gambling, drink, expensive hobbies, and women. Nash had always prided himself on not indulging in such pursuits. However, while he had congratulated himself, and taken care of business in Parliament, he had failed his tenants, his family, his title, and his future heirs. He'd been entrusted with the managing of his estate, and had fallen short.

He turned as Bower spoke again. "I took the liberty of notifying the magistrate of the goings-on. He said he would keep a look out for Jones, but he assumed—probably rightly so—that the man is long gone and will not return."

"How much did Jones pilfer?"

"The closest figure I can come to is somewhere between five and six hundred pounds."

Nash blew out a low whistle. Five or six hundred pounds! Well, he had no one to blame but himself. "That is a good bit of money. I am thinking he had been working in his father's stead for some time. Perhaps the older Mr. Jones had turned over management to his son long before he left to live with his daughter."

If he'd been less sure of the dowry Lady Grace would have brought him, he might have considered that his steward was robbing him—and his tenants—blind.

He returned to his chair, and leaning back, he tented his fingers and explained the details of the investment project he'd involved himself in. Laying out the plan clearly and concisely to his man of business convinced him the investment opportunity had been the right thing to do.

Bowers leaned forward, his appreciation for the investment apparent in his eyes. "That is very good, my lord. Those kinds of ventures tend to pay well. Of course, there are certain risks, as I am sure you are aware."

"Indeed, and in all fairness to Mr. Sueade, who ran the meeting and is setting up the consortium, all of the perils involved in such an undertaking were clearly laid out."

"That is certainly good news, my lord. Perhaps we can recoup some of the damage Mr. Jones has done to your financial state." Bowers began shoving papers into his satchel in preparation to leave.

Nash looked up as Arabella rushed past the open door of the library. She carried some type of animal in her hands.

He sighed. Solve one problem, another crops up.

• • •

Arabella stood next to Lord Honeyfield at the Nightingdale soiree, who was rattling on about his problems with his man of business. Since dancing was never a part of a soiree, merely throngs of people dressed to impress while searching the crowd for something else to gossip about, Arabella decided to seek out the refreshment table. Her appetite had increased over the last couple of weeks, which she could only attribute to settling into her new life.

With Nash engaged in a deep conversation with Lord Blanchard about Parliamentary matters, she excused herself and wandered away. The scent of so many bodies pressed together in the space, along with women's perfume and men's hair tonic, had a dizzying effect on her. She barely made it to the refreshment tables before black dots began to gather in her eyes, and with a gentle swish of skirts, she slid to the ground.

When she awakened, Nash knelt by her side, his face a picture of concern. He reached for a cold cloth from someone's hand that he patted her forehead with. "Are you all right, sweeting?"

She tried to sit up, but his hand on her chest stopped her. "No, don't rise just yet. Give yourself a chance to recover from your swoon."

A circle of curiosity-seekers surrounded her, making her heart pound. She'd never wanted to be the center of attention, and it seemed ever since she'd met this man she was right there. "I never swoon." She huffed.

His grin annoyed her. She'd always been a stalwart sort, chafing at women who collapsed at every occasion. Why, she operated on animals and tended to cuts and gouges that would turn the stomach of some men. She closed her eyes, wishing herself back home in her bedchamber.

"I will escort Lady Clarendon to the retiring room, my lord. A slight rest will do her well. Unless, of course, you wish to take her home." Lady Millerton, an older outspoken harridan of the *ton* leaned over her, directing her comments to Nash.

Wait just a minute. Why was the old biddy speaking about her as if she weren't there? "I feel fine now. Please allow me to get up." Her cheeks burned, and she wanted more than anything to gain her feet and forget this entire incident. Would there never be any peace in her life? Was she to be forever the subject of gossip and speculation?

Nash stood and helped her to her feet. For a moment, she felt as though she might faint again, but clutched his hand until the feeling passed. "I think we should go home, my dear."

Nothing would have made her happier, but she was determined to stay, at least for a little while more. She certainly did not want to give the gossips more fodder for their nastiness. "I am fine. Truly. Perhaps a drink of some sort would help."

Nash studied her. "Are you sure?"

He still had that ridiculous grin on his face, and she failed to see the humor in the situation. "Yes. I am sure."

After leading her to a chair and seeing her settled, he left her to make his way through the crowd to find her a drink. She waved her fan in her face, wishing she had asked him to escort her to the patio outside. An old friend, Lady Voss, who had provided needed but unwanted advice since Arabella's coming out, placed her impressive bottom on the chair alongside her. "Breeding already, eh?"

"What? Oh no—" Arabella stopped and counted in her head. Heavens, she hadn't had her courses since before she and Nash had married. Could that be the explanation for her swooning, increased appetite, and unsettled stomach at the breakfast table?

A baby. A soft smile settled on her lips.

"Ah, I see I am correct." Lady Voss patted her hand.

Was that why Nash kept grinning at her? It rankled that her husband had arrived at that conclusion before she had. Then she drew in a breath as another thought crossed her mind. After the way they'd married, most likely there would be many who would be counting months. Hopefully, the babe would not come early.

Nash returned with a glass of lemonade. "It is not very cold, but it might refresh you, anyway." She wanted to question him then on what she'd just discovered, but kept silent as Lady Voss continued to chatter away.

The older woman seemed to be settled in for the night. Nash touched Arabella's shoulder. "I see Mr. Dennison over there, and I need to speak with him. Will you be all right while I am gone?"

"I will see to your wife." Lady Voss waved him on. "Just do what you need to do, and we will be right here when you return."

Arabella sighed. So now she was a captive. As her companion prattled on, Arabella thought about a baby. She hadn't had time to adjust to marriage, and now she would be faced with a little baby. Oh, how she wished they could return to the country now. The thought of nourishing food, fresh air, and mild exercise in the way of long walks, away from the foul smells of London and the even more constant appraising by the *ton*, left her anxious to speak with her husband.

It seemed an eternity, but actually only about thirty minutes, before Nash returned. "Are you ready to go home?"

All of a sudden, she felt very, very tired. "Yes, I believe I am." Arabella stood and shook out her skirts, bidding Lady Voss a good evening. She took Nash's arm, and they wended their way through the throng.

Since they were leaving as other guests were just arriving, it took a bit of time for their carriage to be brought around. Nash spent the time talking to Lord and Lady Dumont, who were also awaiting their carriage. They were leaving early, Lady Dumont said, because their young son was down with a fever, and even though Nurse was a careful guardian, Lady Dumont felt better returning home.

Another issue that brought concern to Arabella. Children got sick. They fell and injured themselves. Sometimes they died. She shuddered.

"Are you chilled, my dear?" Nash eyed her.

"A bit. I am eager to return home. The crowds and noise are starting to wear on me."

Just then the butler announced their carriage was ready. Nash helped her down the steps and assisted her into the carriage. He sat across from her and tapped on the ceiling to alert the driver to proceed.

Arabella was not quite ready to discuss the possibility of a baby with Nash just yet. Even if he did seem to be aware of her condition—before herself, in fact—she still felt more time needed to pass before she could be assured that she was, indeed, increasing. Once she was certain, she would ask for them to return to the country.

"Arabella, I am sorry you fell ill this evening. I had hoped to talk to you about hosting a dinner party in the near future."

"A dinner party?"

He leaned back and rested his foot on his knee. "Yes. I know you are not fond of these affairs, but we need to solidify our position within the *ton*, which will especially help my work in Parliament. It doesn't have to be a large party. Just ten or so guests."

Lord. Here she was about to ask to have them return to the country, and he wanted her to take on a dinner party with the very people she loathed.

She shook her head. "I do not feel up to a dinner party. Not yet."

"When?"

Attempting to lighten the mood, she said, "Never?"

"It is your duty as a countess to see to our social calendar. That involves hosting parties ourselves." He tugged on the cuffs of his shirt and added, "You always seem to have enough time to forage for injured creatures and attend to them."

She raised her chin. "It so happens I enjoy the company of animals much more than the company of nasty gossipers always looking to find something wrong with me."

The carriage rolled to a stop. "We will discuss this further when you are not so overwrought."

"I am not overwrought."

"Nevertheless, we will continue in the morning."

She gritted her teeth. How she hated when he treated her like a child. She ignored his arm and proceeded up the steps ahead of him. With any luck, she wouldn't ruin her exit by fainting again.

• • •

After two weeks of frantic preparations, Nash joined Arabella in the drawing room as they waited for their dinner guests to arrive. He'd been quite proud of how she had handled the upcoming event. Although she was nervous about hosting her first dinner party, it looked as though everything necessary had been done quite to perfection.

Once she'd consulted with Cook about the menu for the evening, she'd asked him to approve it, as well. For a woman who resented any interference from him on most things, it was rewarding and amusing that she would consult him on this.

He wandered to the side board and poured a brandy. "Would you care for a sherry, sweeting?"

"Yes, please. Perhaps that will help to calm my nerves."

Handing the glass to her, he said, "From what I have seen, you have nothing to be nervous about. The table setting is perfect, and we can certainly count on Cook to present a wonderful meal. We have a nice variety of guests who will keep the conversation going. It will be fine."

He didn't add, since he wanted to keep her spirts up, but she looked exhausted the last couple of weeks. She'd been taking naps, but apparently early pregnancy—which she had yet to mention to him—was taking its toll on her body. In all fairness to her health, and the well-being of the babe, once this dinner party was over, he might suggest they retire to the country.

Quinn arrived at the drawing-room door. "Lord and Lady Templeton have arrived, my lord."

The couple entered the room, followed shortly by Baron Cloverfield and Lady Cloverfield. Within less than twenty minutes, all the guests had gathered in the drawing room, awaiting the dinner announcement.

Nash was proud of Arabella. Even though he knew she was nervous and fatigued, she carried on conversations with their guests and circulated to each group to make sure everyone was comfortable. Even though she didn't believe it, she was an excellent hostess, and so far, everything was going just fine. He would need to compliment her later on about how well she'd handled it all.

Quinn appeared at the drawing room door and announced dinner in his usual perfunctory manner. The guests lined up in order of rank and strolled to the dining room. He had Lady Templeton on his arm, and Arabella was escorted by Lord Templeton.

The seating arrangement had been worked out between the two of them one night as they sat naked on their bed after a rousing session of lovemaking. He had Mrs. Talbot on one side, and Arabella's friend Lady Lovell on the other side. The footmen began serving and pouring the first wine as the dinner began.

As the meal continued, he watched Arabella over the rim of his wine glass and couldn't help smiling. Any residue of nervousness had left her as she had a lively conversation with Lord Lovell. From what he could hear, they were discussing the need for education for the underclass. He shook his head. His wife certainly had Whig leanings.

Before the fourth course had been served, Quinn entered the room and bent to Arabella's ear and spoke softly. She blanched and appeared agitated.

Nash frowned. "What is it?"

She lowered her voice and said, "Apollo got out of the kennel and was run over by a carriage. He needs attention."

"One of the dogs?"

She nodded, biting her lower lip. By this time, they had the attention of most of the guests at the table. Surely, she would not do this to him. Important people sat at their table. For God's sake, they were hosting a dinner party! "I am sure one of the maids can handle it."

"I'm sorry, but I must see to the animal myself. No one else knows how to stitch him up."

Mrs. Talbot put her hand to her chest. "Lady Clarendon, certainly you are not going to tend to an injured animal yourself?" She looked as though she were about to faint.

"No, she will not." Nash glared at her.

Arabella hesitated, then carefully laid her napkin down and stood. "I am sorry. I will return shortly." She avoided Nash's shocked expression as she turned and hurried from the room.

Chapter Nineteen

Later that night, Arabella quietly entered the library. The disaster of the dinner party had ended over an hour before. She had spent the time since then with Apollo, checking on his injures. Earlier, she had sewn him up and doused him with whiskey to help him sleep. It looked as though he would recover.

She had rejoined the dinner party, but Nash's coolness and the other guests' curiosity had made for an unpleasant finish to the event. Maybe things might have ended differently had he supported her decision.

Nash stood at the window, his back to her, sipping on a glass of brandy.

"Quinn asked that I join you?" She moved farther into the room.

He turned to face her. "Please close the door."

Raising her chin, she did as he bid. Once the door was closed, he studied her for a minute, his hands on his hips. "Arabella, this has to stop."

"What?"

He rubbed the back of his neck. "Ever since we married, my life has been in turmoil." He raised his hand as she began to speak. "Please hear me out. I have dealt rather fairly, I believe, with your animal nonsense."

A hard lump descended in Arabella's stomach. Nash looked very serious, and his lowered voice was more reason for concern than if he'd been shouting at her.

"We currently house numerous dogs in the kennel out back that you keep telling me you will find a good home for—soon. Three more animals in various stages of recovery take up one of the bedchambers. At this rate, there will not be room for *us* to even live in this house."

"I know this seems odd—"

"Stop." He walked in a circle, his head down, and then came to stand in front of her, his hands on her shoulders. "I want this all to stop. No more taking in animals. No more surgery. I want you to behave in a manner more fitting of a countess. We need to take our place in Society, and to do that we cannot host dinner parties where the hostess disappears to perform animal surgery. It is your duty as my wife to see to the running of the household and do wife-type things."

"Wife-type things?"

"Yes. Accept afternoon calls. Go on visits yourself. Take a ride in Hyde Park in the afternoon. Go shopping, paint watercolors, embroider things, play the pianoforte. I know you are familiar with the routine of ladies."

"Yes. And I have always hated the routine of ladies." She swept her hand toward the window. "Those ladies hate me. I have never been a darling of the *ton*, but since the entire *ton* believes I snatched you from Lady Grace's clutches, I have become a pariah."

She wiped a tear from her eye. "The one time I enjoyed myself at a ball, we ended up arguing with each other. At the soiree, I fainted, which I am sure has made the rounds of gossips." She threw her hands out. "Why can't you see I don't belong here?"

. . .

Nash stared at her, finally realizing with a sinking feeling that this marriage would never work. He had a position to maintain. Already, word was spreading that his wife was less than a proper countess, and he'd been forced to ignore snide remarks in the halls of Parliament about him running an animal welfare home. In fact, much to his horror, his credibility on a bill he was sponsoring had been questioned.

He'd spent all his life doing the proper thing. Not for him had been the wild life of a young noble. Once finished with University, he'd been discreet with his mistresses, never dallied with a married woman, gambled very little, avoided reckless races in the park at dawn, and rarely drank to excess.

He'd wanted a wife who would do all the things he'd just laid out. And do them with joy. Instead, he had a wife who despised Society, had no intention of taking her place among them, and was only happy when she was up to her elbows in animal blood and chaos. They were too far apart in their way of thinking.

"Then it appears we are at a standstill, my dear," his tone mirrored the sadness in his heart.

She picked up on his tone and echoed it. "So it seems."

The silence was overwhelming. And sad. Hopefully, the child she carried was a male child, and once the heir was born, they could live their separate lives. His heart twisted with the picture he had of his life. Lonely, frustrating, and empty. Despite a separation, he would not break his marriage vows. But how could he continue his life with the constant barrage of turmoil and the humiliation of his wife's behavior? It did not suit him.

"If you wish to retire to the country, I will arrange to have the staff at Clarendon Manor notified of your arrival." He choked on the words.

"My arrival?" The surprise in her voice told him she did not understand what he meant.

"Yes, sweeting. As I've explained to you numerous times, it is necessary for me to be in London, at least until Parliament recesses. It is probably best if you and your animals take up residence at the Manor."

She grew pale, and for a moment he thought she would swoon. But she straightened her shoulders and gave him a half smile. "And you will join us once Parliament recesses?"

Tension hung in the air as he studied her before responding. "I think not. 'Tis for the best if we separate."

Her eyes grew wide, and she placed her hand on her stomach. "I am with child, my lord."

Ah, so now she decided to tell him. Was her revelation a way to make him feel guilty? To reconsider his decision? Arabella was so very different from every other woman he knew in the *ton*. She cared for none of the things most women of her station cared about. He'd spent the last few months trying to figure her out and had reluctantly come to the realization that they were very unsuited to each other. Something she had tried to tell him from the start.

"I know."

Arabella sat, her mouth open. "You know?"

"Yes. I can count." He walked across the room and stared out the window, his hands behind his back. "I was just waiting for you to tell me."

"I only just realized myself a few weeks ago. It appears I am not as good at counting as you are." She offered him a crooked smile.

He shrugged. "I will, of course, attend you when the babe is due. Just send word."

She nodded. "I see." Arabella stood and shook out her skirts. "Then I guess I will inform Sophia to see to the packing."

"I will send word immediately for the staff to expect you."

Without another word, she turned and headed to the door.

"Arabella." He held his hand out.

"What?" She looked at him over her shoulder, tears glistening in her eyes.

"I'm sorry. I just wish…"

She took in a deep breath. "As do I."

• • •

Nash entered White's on a cold and rainy early evening. Arabella and the menagerie had all left for the country two weeks before. He'd thought of nothing else all day, every day, but Arabella. Her smile, her laugh. How her eyes lit up when she talked about her animals.

No matter how hard he tried, he could not sleep without her next to him. Considering he'd slept alone for years, and with her for only a few months, the entire situation was ludicrous. He'd even taken to having warm milk before he retired, certainly a reason to have him banned from his clubs. But, instead of sleeping, he lay on his back, his hands tucked behind his head, staring at nothing, and remembering.

When it became apparent he was not going to enjoy a night's sleep, he would throw off the covers and pace. Pulling on a banyan, he would tie the belt tightly and descend the stairs to the library where he would attempt to read. Books hadn't helped. Brandy hadn't helped. Staring at the flames in the fireplace hadn't helped.

Nash handed his wet greatcoat and hat to Duncan, the longtime butler at the club door. Duncan bowed slightly, and Nash entered the main room. Nearing dinnertime, the club was full with men seeking company, coffee, whiskey, cards, and food. Nash refused to eat one more meal alone. Cook had taken to making several dishes he despised. The way she sniffed when he questioned her on it told him exactly how she felt about Arabella and her circus leaving. He thought to remind her who paid her wages, but feeling uncomfortable himself, he had finally decided to seek his dinner elsewhere.

He took a chair near the back wall and signaled a footman to bring him a brandy. He would have one or two drinks and then make his way to the dining room. He was perusing the evening newspaper when a deep voice interrupted him. "Evening, Clarendon. I haven't seen you in an age."

The Duke of Manchester settled himself across from Nash. He'd always liked the duke and found him to be friendly, but definitely not one to cross. He had five sisters he'd seen married off and was known to be completely, and unabashedly, besotted with his duchess. A duchess who was an acknowledged and respected botanist. Perhaps His Grace was just the person with whom to speak.

"'Tis true, Your Grace. How does your family fare?"

Manchester leaned back and signaled a footman. "Quite well, thank you. Her Grace and I welcomed our new daughter, Lady Bernice, the September past." He pointed to Nash's drink, which the footman noted and returned with a glass of brandy for each of them.

"That is now, what, two daughters and a son?"

"Precisely. I seem to be following in my father's footsteps. One son and the rest daughters. Robert, Marquess of Stratford, Lady Esther, and now Lady Bernice." The pride in the man's voice, and face, had Nash's stomach clenching. If only he and Arabella had come together, he might one day show the same pride in his offspring. The way things looked now, there might be only one.

He pushed the sad thought away. "And Her Grace? She

is well?"

"Indeed, and as busy as ever. Since no nurse or governess seems to suit her for long, she spends a great deal of time with our children, but any free minutes in her day are devoted to her science." Manchester placed his glass on the small table next to him. "How goes your new marriage?"

Nash pasted a fake smile on his face. "Fine. Just fine."

Manchester's raised eyebrows told him he hadn't fooled the duke. "I have heard rumors that Lady Clarendon has retired to the country, yet you remain here."

"Parliament."

The duke continued to stare at him, and Nash blurted out, "How do you accept Her Grace's delving into science? Her a duchess?"

"Ah. Does your wife have some offending hobbies? Have little interest in the usual pursuits of ladies of her station?"

Nash blew out a breath. He needed someone to talk to, and apparently speaking with a man who had dealt with a similar issue might help. "She collects injured animals. Then brings them home and nurses them back to health. My life and home are in chaos."

"So it seems." The duke took a sip of his drink. "Much like my life, it would appear."

Nash relaxed when the duke continued. "I was very upset when my wife and I first married. I thought she showed none of the skills, nor the desire to learn them, that a duchess must possess."

He snorted. "I certainly understand."

Manchester studied the brandy in his glass as he swirled the liquid. "The most difficult moment was when I discovered that against my explicit orders, she had been submitting scientific papers under a man's name to the Linnean Society."

Nash tried very hard not to laugh, but the idea of the meek, easygoing Duchess of Manchester defying the duke was hilarious.

Thinking of his dinner party, he asked, "Did anyone ever find out?"

Manchester threw his head back and laughed. "She was nominated for an award that all of London knew about, and she asked me to accept it for her."

"Lie?" Nash was appalled.

"Oh yes."

He leaned forward, loving the story. "What did you do?"

"After much thought, I agreed to accept the award for her."

Nash shook his head. The story got more interesting. "And what happened?"

"I stood before the entire Linnean Society and told them I was a fake. That my lovely, talented, brilliant wife had duped them all."

He sat back, his mouth agape. "You didn't."

"I did." He grinned. "You see, Her Grace is adored by our staff, and our children are free to climb upon her, sticky hands and all. She has been known to commiserate with a maid over the loss of a beau and help a footman count the silver if the poor man is behind in his duties.

"However, in order to maintain her standing in Society, I will on occasion absolutely insist that we host a dinner party, or soiree. She then manages to rally the staff to do everything that needs to be done in time for the event." He smiled. "She truly amazes me."

It did sound as though the duke's life was as unconventional as Nash's had become. Yet the man seemed happy.

"You are happy?"

His smile grew into a large grin. "Absolutely. I love my wife, and anything that makes her happy does the same for me."

I love my wife.

Why did those words not trouble him as much as they had in the past?

Nash leaned back and considered Manchester's words. The duke took a final sip of his drink. "I am afraid I must leave you now. I see Redgrave across the room, and we are late for a meeting."

He watched Manchester greet his brother-in-law, another devoted husband, and the two of them chatted easily as they left the club. Nash called for another brandy, which he sipped while he considered the duke's words.

Chapter Twenty

Arabella swayed back and forth on the swing hanging from the large oak tree on the south side of Clarendon Manor. She placed her hand on her belly, the slight swell a comfort. How much more she would enjoy the anticipation of a babe if Nash were here with her. She missed him a great deal. In fact, so much so it surprised her. His smile, the way he rubbed the back of his neck or ran his fingers through his hair when he was faced with a dilemma.

Dilemmas that were mostly caused by her.

Had she been selfish in her demands that she be allowed to drag home any number of injured and bleeding animals? Truth be known, she could very well have made some concessions. Had she honestly believed that everything should go her way in marriage? She'd watched her mother host dinner parties, soirees, and Arabella's coming-out ball. It would not be so very difficult for her to do the same for Nash.

He'd allowed her to bring home animals and treat them, commandeering his library, and taking up space in an empty bedchamber. Although she'd promised many times to search for good homes for them, she had been quite remiss in that endeavor.

The only time she had honored his request to host a dinner party, she had humiliated him by leaving their guests to tend to an animal. Feeling guilty and not too proud of herself, Arabella stood and shook out her skirts. She needed a distraction, a way to forget some of the things she'd done to the man who had been honorable enough to marry her to save her reputation when she had no care for it.

Perhaps a ride on her horse, Bessie, would be just the thing. She slowly climbed the stairs and entered her bedchamber. Before she pulled out her riding habit, she crossed the room and opened the door leading to Nash's bedchamber. That was another thing that troubled her. She was having a most difficult time sleeping.

She loved pushing her bottom up against Nash and having him wrap his strong arm around her middle and pulling her close. She'd felt secure and protected. Cared for. Two weeks away from Nash seemed like so much more. How could someone crawl into her heart so easily?

Crawl into my heart?

She moaned, knowing the truth of it. As she sat on her bed, she considered the situation. She was carrying a babe, and wanted—nay needed—her husband with her. To share in the joy of the first fluttering in her tummy, to talk about names, dream about their child, and argue over godparents. True, he'd banished her to the country, but it had been her choice to leave.

Sighing, she stood and rang the bell for Sophia. Once she was outfitted in her riding habit, she strode from the house to the stables. Martin, the head stable master, pushed his cap back on his head and offered her a bright smile. "Will you be needing a groom to accompany you this morning, my lady?"

"No. I won't be leaving the property."

She placed her foot in his hand, and he hoisted her onto the horse. She had a moment's dizziness, but then shook her head to clear it.

"Are you well, my lady?"

"Yes. I am fine. Thank you." She tapped Bessie and the mare took off. She gave the horse her head and enjoyed the wind whipping through her hair. Pretty soon, she would not be able to ride this way, but she did not have Nash here to order her about.

Her hat flew from her head, and she laughed as it landed on a pile of leaves. She continued on, the fresh air in her lungs helping to clear the cobwebs from her head.

When she returned from her ride, she would pen a note to Nash and inquire after his well-being. She hadn't received any correspondence from him, but one of them had to make the first move. Her heart felt lighter, and for the first time in two weeks, some hope of future happiness filled her.

One thing she could do while she waited for his response was to find homes for several of the dogs. It would hurt to give away some of them, but Nash was more important than animals. It was a shame it had taken her so long, and a separation, to realize that.

She climbed a rise and slowed the horse to a trot, then a walk. From here she could see the entire estate, all the tenants' cottages, and the village off to the east, smoke from the chimneys floating in the air. Nash's new land steward had been doing a wonderful job of meeting with the tenants, discerning their needs, and assuring them Lord Clarendon was truly interested in their success. Probably the best news he'd granted them was an end to the rent increase Jones had put into place.

The man still had not been found, but when she'd spoken with the new steward, Mr. Nelson, he had assured her he kept in touch with the magistrate to make sure Jones was still being sought.

She continued to take in the view and inhaled a deep breath of the country air. As much as she loved it here, her place was with her husband. Instead of writing and waiting for a response, she would pack up and return to London. The animals could stay here, and as much as it would break her heart, she would ask the staff to find homes for them. Once in London, she would limit her walks in the park so she wasn't confronted by so many injured animals. She would, however, at least still help those who wandered into her path.

She would even—she shuddered—host another dinner party with orders she was not to be disturbed.

For any reason.

Feeling lighthearted and good about her decision, and anxious to begin the process of packing and returning to Town, she pulled on the reins and turned Bessie. Tapping the side of the animal with her crop, they took off, bounding down the hill toward the manor.

The first thing she would do when she returned to London was to tell Nash that he meant more to her than the animals. He had captured her heart. She grinned at the thought and hoped it wasn't too late. He had tried to reason with her, but she'd been stubborn about doing everything her way. No more.

A slight niggling of doubt crept into her thoughts. Had he already given up on her? Would he turn her away when she returned? Chewing on her lip and pondering Nash's response, she neglected to steer Bessie away from the rabbit hole. The horse stumbled, and Arabella went flying through the air, landing with a thump on her hip. Dazed, she sat up, then stood. A wave of nausea and dizziness washed over her, and she felt a stickiness between her legs.

Her knees buckled, and she landed back on the ground.

My baby!

• • •

Nash was finishing up his correspondence in preparation for leaving for Clarendon Manor. He would put a few hours on the road today, spend the night at an inn, and reach the Manor tomorrow. It had been a good decision.

After Manchester had left him the prior evening, Nash had sat and considered his situation. Yes, Arabella was stubborn. Yes, Arabella enjoyed taking care of injured animals. Yes, Arabella disdained Society and was not what he'd planned on when he'd decided to take a wife.

But she *was* his wife. Their two weeks apart had convinced him he did not want to live without her. Her deep commitment to helping those in need spoke a great deal about her character. So, she was not a frivolous miss, who lived to attend parties, and talk about styles and gossip, and cut other young ladies down. There was not a mean bone in the woman's body.

That was what he loved about her. And love her he did. As Manchester had said, if it made her happy, then it would make him happy, as well. Who needed a well-run house, anyway? He chuckled at the thought as Quinn entered the library. "My lord, a messenger has arrived from Clarendon Manor."

A messenger? "Send him in."

"My lord." The man Nash recognized as a lesser groom at Clarendon Manor entered the room, his hat in his hand. He held out a missive that Nash took and read. All the blood left his face, and he tried to control his breathing.

Lady Clarendon took a spill from her horse. May lose the babe.

It had been signed by his housekeeper. Numb for a moment, he recovered himself and addressed the groom. "Go to the kitchen and have Cook fix you something to eat." He turned to his man of business. "An emergency has come up, and I must leave immediately for the country."

"What about the rest of the correspondence? And I have a very promising report from the man who is running the venture you invested in. While I would not say your financial problems are over, they are certainly much less dire than they had been."

Despite the good news, Nash was anxious to be on his way. "Pack it up and bring all of it with you to the Manor. Take my carriage. I will be riding one of the stable horses."

He left the room and instructed Quinn to have Andrews pack him an overnight bag and to notify the stables that he will need one of the sturdier horses saddled and ready to leave post haste.

May lose the babe.

The words echoed in his brain as he changed into riding clothes and made ready to leave. Arabella must be terrified. And alone.

What a fool I've been.

• • •

The two-day trip turned into ten hours with Nash only allowing himself stops at inns along the way to switch horses and eat a quick meal. He was tired and scruffy when he rode over the rise before Clarendon Manor. He paused for a moment, which he did whenever he arrived home. The sight of the place he'd been raised, and where generations of Lords Clarendon had lived, always caused his heart to swell.

He rubbed the back of his neck, not sure what he would find, then kicked the horse to finish his journey, riding into the stable. With a quick nod to the stable master, he jumped from the horse, tossed the reins to the man's outstretched hand, and headed to the house.

All was quiet when he entered. "Good evening, my lord."

Nash nodded at the butler at the door, a new man. "Is her

ladyship in her bedchamber?"

"Yes, my lord. I believe the surgeon is with her now."

His lips tight, Nash bounded up the stairs. He knocked lightly on the door and entered. Arabella lay in bed, apparently asleep. She was pale, her lustrous hair spread over the pillow where her head rested. The surgeon spoke with Sophia, who turned at his entrance. "Oh my lord. Thank heavens you are here."

Suddenly his mouth dried up, fearing what he would hear. Gritting his teeth, he moved toward the bed. "How is she?"

The surgeon smiled. "This is my second visit. Her ladyship bruised her hip when she fell, which is a minor concern. My fear had been for the babe she told me she was carrying."

Nash nodded and held his breath as he waited for the man to continue. "She has had some bleeding, but as of this morning, it has stopped. If it does not start up again, I think the babe will be fine."

Nash released the breath and tears flooded his eyes. He wanted to drop to his knees and thank God, but right now he needed more information. He swallowed several times to keep the tears from falling. "And she is well?"

"Yes. Only a bruised hip. But she was very lucky. A fall like this in her condition could have been quite catastrophic."

"Nash?" Arabella's weakened voice called to him from the bed. "You came." Her smile lit up her face, causing him to grin.

"Yes, sweetheart. I came as soon as I received word of your accident."

She rested her hands on her stomach. "The doctor thinks the baby might be all right."

He walked to the bed and sat alongside her, taking her hand in his. "Yes, he just told me." He kissed her hand and rested her palm on his face. "How do you feel?"

"Tired. I have been given something to sleep since the

doctor thought sleep and bed rest might keep the babe in place."

He studied her for a minute, taking in the lavender and lemon scent that followed her everywhere. She looked tired and wan, but never more beautiful to him. How he had missed her, and how much he wanted to make things right between them.

"I want to—"

They both started at once. However, what he wanted to say required privacy. He looked over his shoulder at the surgeon and Sophia. "If you will leave us now, I would like to speak with her ladyship in private."

The surgeon nodded. "I have given instructions to her lady's maid. If you have any questions, please send a note around and I will return. Right now, it looks as though all is well as long as her ladyship remains in bed for at least two weeks."

"I guarantee it, sir." He turned to Arabella. "Even if I have to tie her to the bed."

The surgeon coughed slightly, and he and Sophia left the room.

Nash looked down at Arabella who looked uneasy, as though she were afraid of what he intended to say. He rubbed his suddenly wet palms on his pants. "There are several things we need to discuss."

· · ·

Arabella couldn't believe Nash was really here. She had thought about him, and prayed that he would come to her, so much so, that when he'd first entered the room, she was afraid her tired mind had conjured him up from her imagination.

He looked so good. Scruffy, with red-rimmed eyes and his clothes full of road dust. He studied her with such concern in his eyes, she imagined perhaps he returned her feelings. Could she be so fortunate that he had discovered during their separation that he wanted her as much as she wanted him?

"I'm sorry—"

Again, they both spoke at the same time. Nash held up his hand. "No, I go first." He took both of her hands in his and kissed her knuckles, gazing into her eyes as he spoke. "I love you, Arabella. The last two weeks have been terrible, the worst time of my life. I miss you, your smile, your laughter, and yes, the craziness that is our life.

"As I have now joined the ranks of to-be-pitied besotted husbands, I will no longer complain about your animals. I want you to be happy, sweetheart, and if being up to your elbows in animal blood"—he shuddered—"makes you happy, then it will make me happy, as well."

Arabella swallowed the sob threatening to erupt from her chest. "And I love you, Nash." She continued in a thick voice, fighting the tears. "It only took a few days here by myself to realize I care about you and our marriage more than I ever will about animals. I was planning to come back to London to host another dinner party"—she shuddered—"and be the perfect *ton* wife when I was thrown from Bessie."

"Ah, sweeting, you are the perfect *ton* wife for me." He leaned over and kissed her gently on the lips. "The best thing that ever happened to me was you falling into my arms in a dark library at the Ashbourne's ball. I thought I wanted a typical debutante for a wife. You showed me that what I considered a typical wife would make me bored and restless for the rest of my life."

Despite her best effort, a lone tear slid down her cheek. "I am giving away most of the dogs in the kennel. The staff has been finding homes for them since I've been bedridden."

She released the rest of the tears that were trying so hard to burst forth. He pulled her up and hugged her to his chest. "We will each make some concessions, and I'm not promising that we won't argue over things, but in the long run, what matters is we love each other, and we can overcome whatever difficulties we face."

Nash stretched out on the bed alongside Arabella. "I am exhausted." He intertwined their fingers together. "I haven't slept well since you left."

"Me, neither."

He tapped her on the nose. "I miss your warm bottom shoved up against my hip."

Arabella felt the heat rise to her face. "My lord!"

Nash yawned and turned on his side. "I need food, but I'm too tired to go to the kitchen and interrupt Cook to make me something."

"My lady, is there anything else you need for the night?" Sophia entered the room and stopped abruptly when she saw Nash lying alongside Arabella on the bed. "Oh, excuse me, my lord." She began to back out.

Nash sat up. "No, wait. Don't leave."

She continued to ease herself toward the door. "My lord?"

"Yes. I am in dire need of sustenance. Please see what you can find in the kitchen. Bread, cheese, fruit, anything at all."

"Yes, my lord." She still looked uncomfortable with the two of them in bed together. "My lady, do you wish something as well?"

"Bring enough for both of us. Her ladyship needs food." He rested his hand on her belly. "A great deal of food."

Sophia smiled. "Yes, my lord."

"And tea."

Once the door closed, Nash drew the covers off Arabella and ran his hand over her slight belly. He bent and kissed her stomach. "Good night, little one. Soon you will become part of the most peculiar family in all of Christendom."

Arabella's brows rose. "Only Christendom, my lord?"

He smiled her favorite crooked smile, warming her heart. "Give us time, my love, just give us time."

Epilogue

"Sweetheart, calm down. The dinner party will be fine. You have everything all planned out. Please don't fret." Nash pulled Arabella into his arms, trying desperately to soothe her. Perhaps, given her condition, he should not have allowed her to take this on, but once they'd returned from the country, she had insisted she could do it.

This time a full month had gone into the planning. He had suggested she summon her mother from Bath to assist, but Arabella declined, seeming to want to prove something. Either to him or herself.

He had joined her in her bedchamber, where Sophia was putting the finishing touches on her hair. Arabella looked beautiful, her pregnancy giving her skin a creamy glow. Her slight belly showed beneath her pale rose gown, reminding him that once this party ended, they would be heading back to Clarendon Manor.

Parliament had recessed, and he was anxious to get

Arabella away from the hot, humid London air. He swore every day the smell from the Thames got worse. He would have to give some serious thought to the future. As much as he enjoyed serving in Parliament, he was reluctant to bring his family back to Town. He'd learned from their short separation that living apart was not for him.

They spoke of their trip back to the country as they descended the steps to the drawing room. Nash poured a brandy for him and a sherry for Arabella. They had only just taken their seats when there was a loud screech, followed by shouting. A small critter raced into the room with one of Arabella's cats chasing the thing. Behind them was one of the downstairs maids waving a feather duster in her hand.

"My lord, catch the cat," Arabella hopped up and shouted.

"Catch him?" Dear God, he was dressed for a dinner party, and his wife wanted him to catch a cat? One look at the frantic look on Arabella's face was enough for him. "Certainly, I will catch him."

"Her."

"Yes. Of course." The critter and the cat had vanished under the settee, so Nash got down on his knees and looked, only to have the mouse run at him. Startled, he jumped back and landed on his arse. The mouse ran around the room, the cat on its tail. The maid climbed onto a chair, screeching to raise the dead. The mouse stopped and hovered in the corner near the window. Just as Nash lunged at the cat, the obviously terrified mouse raced toward him and up his body. A loud wail came from the cat, robbed of his treat, who sailed through the air and landed on Nash's chest.

The cat's claws latched onto Nash's cravat, where it hung long enough for him to sneeze several times. He pulled the cat free and let him go.

"I got him!" Quinn stood at the door, his hands cupped around the mouse.

Arabella stared at Nash wide-eyed. "Oh dear."

"What?" He sneezed again.

"Isn't this how it all started?"

Nash pulled on the cuffs of his shirt and dusted off his waistcoat. "Not quite, my love. We're missing the mud." He drew out his handkerchief and blew his nose.

"My lord, Lord and Lady Slade have arrived." Quinn still held the mouse in his hand. The cat had given up the chase and sat patiently licking herself.

Straightening his cravat, Nash walked up to Arabella, extending his aristocratic arm. "Are you ready to greet your guests, my love?"

Arabella stared at him for a moment, then burst out laughing. Resting her hand on his arm, she shook her head. "My lord, you are as addlebrained as the rest of us. Welcome to the club." She smiled as they walked toward the entrance hall, Lord and Lady Clarendon, their heads held high, ready to greet their guests.

Acknowledgments

No book would be complete without input and knuckle rapping from my fabulous editor, Erin Molta. I could never do it without you.

As always, the wonderful authors from the Beau Monde RWA group are so helpful when I'm stuck for a word to use, or need information on the Regency period.

I love the support from my family, who leave me alone when they know I'm struggling, and my daughter who stops in my office every morning after her nightshift and shares her very humorous sarcasm with me. I've used many of her one-liners in my books.

My twin grandsons, otherwise known as the "Twinadoes," are the light of my life. When I'm worn out from trying to find the right way to say something, I take the five-minute drive to my son and daughter-in-law's house and am immediately cheered up. Thank you, Jessica and Scott for sharing your wonderful boys with "Bamma."

About the Author

Callie Hutton, the *USA Today* bestselling author of *The Elusive Wife*, writes both Regency and western historical romance with "historic elements and sensory details" (The Romance Reviews). Callie lives in Oklahoma with several rescue dogs and her top cheerleader husband of many years. Her family also includes her daughter, son, and daughter-in-law. And twin grandsons, "The Twinadoes."

Callie loves to hear from readers. Contact her directly at calliehutton11@gmail.com or find her online at www.calliehutton.com. Sign up for her newsletter to receive information on new releases, appearances, contests, and exclusive subscriber content. Visit her on Facebook, Twitter, and Goodreads.

Get Scandalous with these historical reads...

ENCHANTING THE EARL
a *Townsends* novel by Lily Maxton

Llynmore Castle is the only place Annabel Lockhart has ever considered home. But now there's a new earl, as arrogant as he is handsome, and he wants her gone. If he thinks she'll go quietly, though, he's in for a surprise. Theo Townsend wants to be left alone, but he can't just throw the spirited woman out. Maybe if he frustrates Annabel enough, she'll leave on her own...

THE GENTLEMAN'S PROMISE
a *Daughters of Amhurst* novel by Frances Fowlkes

A social pariah, Lady Sarah Beauchamp yearns for redemption to marry. The assistance of Mr. Jonathon Annesley gives her hope of success. Offering a gentleman's promise to help his sister's friend regain the favor of the *ton* should be easy. After all, he's well liked and considered a rising star in Parliament. Until he learns Sarah's ultimate goal is a husband. She is not for him — his focus rests on gaining political reforms. Yet, a promise made cannot be broken...

ACCIDENTALLY COMPROMISING THE DUKE
a *Wedded by Scandal* novel by Stacy Reid

Miss Adeline Hays is out of options. Determined to escape marriage to a repugnant earl, Adel plans to deliberately allow herself to be caught in a compromising position at a house party with the much kinder man she'd hoped to marry. Instead, Adeline accidentally enters the wrong chamber and tumbles into the bed of the mad duke.

Made in the USA
San Bernardino, CA
15 April 2017